The Woman in the Snow

F. D. Brant

F. D. Brant

GRESHAM, OREGON

Copyright © 2017 by **F. D. Brant**

All rights reserved. No part of this publication may be reproduced, distributed or transmitted in any form or by any means, without prior written permission.

F. D. Brant
P O Box 522
Gresham Or 97030
www.fdbrant.com

Publisher's Note: This is a work of fiction. Names, characters, places, and incidents are a product of the author's imagination. Locales and public names are sometimes used for atmospheric purposes. Any resemblance to actual people, living or dead, or to businesses, companies, events, institutions, or locales is completely coincidental.

Book Layout © 2017 BookDesignTemplates.com

The Woman in the Snow/ F. D. Brant. – 2nd ed.
ISBN 978-1-946179-03-6

This is dedicated to my wife who must put up with this writer and all his quirks.

Acknowledgements:

Scripture quotes are from the NIV Study Bible

Copyright 1985 by Zandervan Corp.

Saturday

Cathy slowly awoke and found herself in an awkward position, *have I fallen out of bed*? If this was so it was the first time since she was very young. What had awakened her anyway? Then she realized that it was very dark and very cold, and it appeared that she was dressed. So she couldn't be in her room. At the same time she realized that her bladder was aching. Maybe that was what had brought her to life. She shifted a little and then realized that just about every muscle in her body hurt. *What did I do?* As she shifted something moved across her chest, and then she realized that it was a seatbelt. Had she been in an accident and had she been knocked unconscious? That thought almost caused her to panic.

Then it came back to her in a flash. That probably was exactly what had happened. She remembered driving down the remote backcountry road eager to get where she was going, and realized that the sky had become ominous, as it appeared that a new snowstorm was approaching rapidly. She could sense that it was getting colder. The storm was something she hadn't expected or prepared for. After all one had just ended and it was very late in the winter so she thought that the one that had just left was the final storm. So she was eager to get on the road and see her fiancé who was ending a semester in college and lived just about a day away.

Looking at the developing storm she became worried, and then she had hit that black ice which immediately sent her car spinning. She remembered desperately trying to get the car back in control and saw the edge of the road coming up quickly. She screamed when she saw that there was no way she was going to stop the car from leaving the road. She felt the car fly off the road and knew that she was in the air. Grabbing the steering wheel desperately she braced herself and found that she put out a quick prayer to be safe. Now, if she didn't hurt as much as she did she would have laughed. While her family, and even her fiancé were Christians, deep in their faith, she thought it was stupid, something that belonged to those first century people. It had nothing to do with anyone who had any ability to truly think. After all, these religions had all been created when man had created gods to solve their problems and things they did not comprehend or understand.

So why did I pray? She remembered her dad stating that there were no unbelievers in the foxhole, and thought maybe when she faced a possibility of death that she like those soldiers just reached out. Well as far as she could see she was alive, but how long had she been unconscious? "Well, Cath' you really did it this time. After all, didn't mom and dad warn you not to leave, as there could easily be another storm. But no you just would not listen . . . you just had to go, impatiently really wanting to see Keith." Cathy, looking around continued talking to herself, "Now my impatience has put me here, and I don't even know where here is?" She knew that her parents had always told her that her impatience would get her into serious trouble someday. But she always had just laughed it off and would say that it never had so she didn't think that it ever would. But now the reality of the situation hit her. She knew that finally it had come back to haunt her. She was in serious trouble and there was a great chance that she could still die out here. She could feel the panic climbing inside of her again, and had to fight to keep in control. If she panicked she knew it would be over.

Then she found herself shaking from the realization of her situation and she started to cry as the emotion of what had just happened surfaced. It lasted only a couple of minutes, but she felt somewhat better. It was really dark, so very dark, and she really hadn't tried to move as of yet – but knew that shortly she would have to. It was her bladder that had brought her back to consciousness. So she must have been unconscious for a few hours. The next thing she realized was that her pants were wet, and wondered if maybe her period had started. It was then she realized that it really couldn't have been since it had ended just two weeks earlier. Although the dampness she felt was similar and just as uncomfortable as if she had started and be caught unprepared. She then thought that maybe the soda she had been drinking that was in the center console spilled on her during the accident. But again feeling the console she found the large cup still there. So how did she get wet? Well the only explanation was simply that in the fear and panic of the crash she had wet herself . . . probably not a surprise. She then smiled a little as it brought up that comment that many mothers always make, "Make sure that you have on clean underwear just in case you get into an accident". She suspected that what had happened to her probably was a common occurrence, so in the end it wouldn't have mattered.

How long had she been unconscious? She just didn't know. Looking around in the darkness she thought, *I guess I had better try and open the door to see where I am.* Reaching down for the door handle she gritted her teeth in pain. As she slowly moved it seemed that she hurt just about everywhere. This panicked her again as she thought maybe that it was blood and not urine she was feeling. But as she checked herself out she could find nothing that would indicate an open wound. So her conclusion about wetting herself was probably the most accurate. Gingerly she again reached for the door handle and tried to open the door. It wouldn't budge. She knew that the car must have ended far down the embankment before coming to rest, as she remembered that there had been a large drop off where she went off the road. There were many large trees, and if she remembered right, a stream that ran under the roadway at this point.

At least she was thankful that her car hadn't landed in the stream. If it had she probably would have either drowned or died from exposure. While it was cold inside the car it was at least bearable. It was at this moment she realized the car was slanted with the passenger side of the car uphill and her side downhill. *Could the car continue to slide? Could she still end up in the water?* With those thoughts the panic tried to rise again, but again she fought it down. The next thought was – *why is it so dark?* About this time that bladder reminded her that she needed to take care of that need or it might just take care of it itself. She leaned forward and realized that she still had the seat belt on and could feel the deflated airbag. These were probably the reasons she was still alive, and presently she seemed to be trapped inside her car.

"Well, I guess I had better see if I can move . . . hmm . . . ouch!" She really did hurt, but again checking herself over there didn't appear to be anything broken just the soreness in every muscle and joint. She was now sure that if she could look herself over that most likely she would be black and blue just about everywhere. "Okay, I guess I had better start trying to get into the back seat. From there I can drop down part of the seat and reach into the trunk and get something to change into so I am not in anything wet.

I think staying in such things with this weather would not be smart." Yet the thought of moving and bringing the pain back was something she did not look forward too. But at the same time just sitting here would not be helpful either. Finally getting up the courage to move she said, "Okay, just take it slow girl, just don't make any quick moves and then it might not hurt so much."

Suddenly, in her mind, flashed the 23rd Psalm. "Now where did that come from?" She asked herself. Then she remembered that her mother had loved plaques and had them all over the house. Each had some scripture written on them. She had seen them all her life and probably had unconsciously memorized each and every one of them. This plaque was by the front door leading out of the house so that it would be a reminder to all of them when they entered into the real world. "I guess in a way it is something appropriate at this time, but there just isn't any god, and if I am going to survive this I will have to just do it on my own, and hope someone finds me soon."

She unhooked her seatbelt and then as she reached across to the passenger side of the car she hit that large empty cup that had held her drink and thought — *I can use that to pee into. After all it's larger than the ones the doctors require you to fill and then I can probably set it in the trunk so it doesn't stink up the car.* Grabbing the cup she put it on the floor in the back area and reached all the way to the door on the passenger side of the car, and then reached down and released the lever and pushed the passenger seat down flat. She then did the same thing with her seat, and slowly crawled over the two seats into the back seat. Once there she then released both seats back to their upright positions, and then dropped the rear seat down in the back so she could reach into the trunk and grab her overnight bag.

As she did this a blast of very cold air came into the car and she could see some light out the trunk, which meant that the trunk lid had sprung open and was exposed to the outside air. Shivering from the difference in temperature she grabbed her bag and then remembered that her dad had made her put a backpack in her trunk that he had put together telling her, "Now Cathy this is an emergency pack. It's a backpack so that if you have to carry it, you can. It has an emergency blanket, flashlight and extra batteries, some food and other things that will help in an emergency. And of course there is lots of water in there – in fact just about a gallon. I know that it's heavy because of that, but sometimes it is something that you really need and may not be available at all." She just shook her head and reluctantly put it in her trunk and then promptly forgot about it. Now she was glad that she had it, as it might just be the difference between being alive after this was all over, or dead. "Thank you daddy", she whispered. "Thank you so much." The emotions began to rise again and she found that the tears were now flowing freely. So much was against her now. Would she, could she have the strength to live through this?

The brief time that she had the rear seat down she could see that it was dark and snowing heavily while she looked through the partially open trunk. She guessed that from the amount she was seeing that her car was probably covered in a blanket of white hiding it completely from any who might come looking for her. Again she knew that the families wouldn't be even worried about her as of yet since she wasn't to be at Keith's family home until late tonight, and she figured it was probably just past dark so she wasn't due to arrive for a few hours yet. Shivering from the cold that she had let into the car she again was thankful that when the trunk had popped partly open that it had not lost her overnight bag and emergency backpack. Quickly opening the backpack she found the emergency blanket and wrapped around her so that she could get warm. Then once a little warm she removed her damp pants and undergarments. The car was leaning with the driver's side facing down; front to rear it seemed to be somewhat level. So before replacing her wet clothes she leaned against the back door on the passenger's side and used the cup to relieve herself, and immediately felt the warmth as the cup filled with her urine. "You know that was something I had never thought about that urine is my body temperature, and I must admit that it sure feels good on my cold hands."

She found that she had almost filled it, and knew that she would need to place it back in the trunk so that the pungent odor wouldn't stink up the car too much. Still, with the heat, she thought that maybe that she would just hold it until her hands got warm, and besides once she opened the car to the trunk again she would lose more heat. While the emergency blanket helped in keeping her warm, she was naked from the waist down, and the drafts that were hitting her were very cold. Yet she didn't want to put down the warm urine, as it was something that felt really good on her cold hands. Finally as it cooled she went ahead and covered it and placed the full container into the trunk again feeling the blast of cold air entering the car. Because she was still naked from the waist down she really felt the cold as it settled on the floor. Quickly now that her hands were free she dug out fresh dry clothes and decided since it was very cold that she would double her undergarments and put on some pantyhose to help keep her warm. She hadn't packed any long underwear so this would have to do for now. While these additional underclothes were somewhat uncomfortable she thought it was better to be uncomfortable than to be freezing.

Now as she warmed slightly, once again, she found the flashlight in the backpack and began to see what was in this kit her dad had made her put in the trunk of her car. Because she really never paid that close attention to what daddy had told her, and if she remembered correctly she had just rolled her eyes thinking – *why would I ever need anything like this? But to humor him I'll just do it.* Now she had to admit that she was quite happy that she hadn't taken it out of the trunk as she had thought to do a number of times. She almost smiled when she thought that this was almost like opening a Christmas gift and discovering what was on the inside. She found that her father had thought this out and there was much here that could help her survive, and survive she must. After all, she had her whole life ahead of her and she did not want it to end here. Again with this thought the emotions began to rise again. She fought to get herself back in control and then once back in control looked back to what she had been doing. One of the first things she found was a basic survival book – something that she did not expect at all. "Wow, he really did plan these packs out." Continuing her search she then found a number of candles, waterproof matches, lighters, a small camp stove that operated on a small propane tank, a hiker's cooking kit, a number of energy tabs, a first aid kit, some MRE's, and stuff that would help her build a fire. Of course there was water in the regular water bottles she was familiar with, but also included was a belt that they would attach to. There was also a mirror, extra batteries, a compass, and a handi-talkie with a note saying for her to use it sparingly as they would go through batteries rather quickly, and to keep it set on 12 –12. If something ever happened then all would be aware of the setting and try to contact each other on that frequency. Without thinking, she set the handi-talkie on the rear shelf so she could grab it quickly if she heard anything on it. Of course when she turned it on, this wouldn't be often.

Right now probably staying with the car was a great idea, so she settled down for an uncomfortable night with at least a candle to help keep the darkness at bay while she was awake, and the emergency blanket to help keep her warm. *Maybe tomorrow with the light of day things will look better.* She had tried the interior light of the car and it didn't work so all she could assume was that the battery had been damaged during the accident. And truly that was not a surprise as the battery was located in the front of the car. She remembered her dad pointing it out to her. So the only light she had came from either the flashlight or the candles. Conserving the flashlight's batteries was important, as she really had no idea how long she would be here. She hoped that it would only be this night, but she could not put her faith in that at all. She also had tried her cell phone and had gotten the no service icon on the phone. Since the car battery had been destroyed her "On Star" system was also dead. So there would be no signal identifying her location. She was driving about 500 miles that day and when they found out that she hadn't arrived that would be a great distance to cover just to find her. As she thought these things through she could feel the panic trying to rise in her again, but realized that allowing it to take control would lessen her chances of getting out of this mess alive. At this point, if she wanted to be real, it probably meant that there was a good chance that it might be days before anyone found her. And until this storm stopped no one could really search anyway. She knew from past experience that the road she traveled had been closed a number of times because of snow.

Finally exhausted both from the drive and the ordeal she had just survived; she attempted to sleep on the back seat, with her head up towards the passenger side of the car, and her feet against the driver side. Not comfortable at all, but at least she was out of this nasty weather and somewhat warm. *Well not exactly warm, but at least I'm not shivering.* She idly wondered how the wild animals dealt with this, but since she was basically a city kid, she had really never been interested in such a thing as animals surviving in the outdoors or in the depth of winter weather.

* * *

Exhausted after her drive she was very happy to see the familiar road leading up to the home of her fiancé's family. Shortly she would be knocking on the door and see the happy faces, and she knew that if there would be a mirror located in the foyer that her face would be the same. The trip had left her tired but exhilarated as in moments she would be in the arms of the one she loved and planned to spend the rest of her life with. As she entered the house it was warm and comfortable here and she could smell something cooking in the kitchen as the smells permeated the house. Keith's mother Jan offered her a cup of coffee and his father suggested that she come in and sit down, and then laughed saying, "Yeah I know, you've been sitting for the last 10 hours." Laughing a little at the small joke she then heard someone coming down from the upstairs and knew it had to be Keith.

Excitement surged through her, as she hadn't seen him in at least a month. He was finishing college and had to concentrate totally on finishing and had jokingly said that if she had been around that he probably would have failed his final classes, as she was just too much of a distraction. Of course she had to ask, "And what kind of distraction would I be?"

Laughing he replied, "Oh, the best kind, but we will have the rest of our lives to be distracted by each other."

Looking expectantly at the stairs she heard Jim say, "Ah I see . . . guess we won't get a chance to do much catching up until the two of you do. Well Cathy, don't just stand there go and spend time with Keith, we'll catch up later."

Smiling back at Keith's father she asked, "Was I that obvious?"

"Yes, you were, now go and we all will talk later."

* * *

She woke up cold, close to shivering, and could hear the wind blowing hard. She then realized that what had just happened was a dream and she was still in this very dangerous situation. All of a sudden she found herself crying deeply. She had just lived in her dream what she had been anticipating and Keith had been so close. But even in the dream she did not get a chance to see him. She wondered if she would ever again. And with that thought started crying even harder. Finally crying herself out she found that it had drained her both emotionally and physically, and before she knew it she had fallen back to sleep.

Sunday – Early Morning to Early Afternoon – Cathy

If she had any more dreams she didn't remember. But when daylight came, the winds had subsided and it looked like the snow was beginning to slow down. There was a chance that it might quit soon. She found that even with the emergency blanket and all the clothes she put on that she was quite cold, and very uncomfortable. It seemed that the winds had pulled whatever heat had been with her right out of the car. She hoped that with the daylight that her family and Keith, with his, would have become worried enough with her not arriving, to get the word out that she was missing. But again with the storm they may have assumed that she had stopped somewhere to wait it out. In truth she felt as if she hadn't slept at all, but knew that even with the starts and stops and periods awake that at least she did sleep some. Then she remembered something else her mother used to say. "When you have reached rock bottom, and despair seems to overwhelm, and there appears to be no way out, that is when God will help. What I mean is that you must give up and then give it to God, or let go and let God."

Again like so many other things all she would do is shake her head at such ignorance. That brought back to her the crash. She remembered saying a quick prayer. Why? Was it because all of her life she had been surrounded by this faith and that some of it had penetrated and become part of her? Having led a protected life she had never been in a situation like she now faced so she thought that she was about to find out what she was really made of. The prospects of survival here were small. And until the storm quit and the snowplow could come out and clear the roads she would be completely on her own. Did she have enough fortitude, strength, and should she say it, *faith* to last?

She had yet to get out of her car and really see what had happened, but knew that she would remain here until it quit snowing. She had opened the rear seat briefly to look through the trunk to the outside and found that the snow appeared to be almost to the level of that trunk. It looked like this new and unexpected storm had dumped a couple of feet of new snow – not a good thing at all for her. She had to assume that the upper side of her car was completely buried and would appear to be nothing more than another snow drift among the many along this road. This depressed her tremendously. How was anyone going to find her? She just had to survive . . . just really survive as she had her whole life ahead of her and didn't want it to end now with her marriage to Keith so close.

The morning seemed endless and the day just dragged. Finally, towards what she assumed to be the early afternoon, the snow quit. Yet the skies remained ominously gray without much form or promise that the storm was ending. Looking at her meager supplies she knew that if the storm didn't clear soon she would completely out of everything that had been placed in that emergency backpack from her father. Plus add in the fact that once again she had to go to the bathroom didn't help. This time she would have to leave the car as liquid elimination was not the problem, but she really didn't want to defecate there in the car. There were plenty of trees to lean against, and she thought that if she used the cup for urine while getting rid of the other she probably could keep her pants at least on around her legs. Now it would be finding a place where the snow wasn't so deep that when she crouched that her behind was sitting in the snow. Not a pleasant thought at all, as right now at this time, she was always cold. Not dangerously so, but uncomfortable anyway. After seeing the snow holding off and the urge growing she knew it would be now or never.

She knew that the driver's door was blocked and had earlier tried the backdoor and found that it at least with some complaint would open. So steeling up the nerve she put the emergency blanket over her shoulders and with some wipes that were included in that kit she carefully exited her wrecked car, and saw that it sat just about at the bottom of the embankment where it had left the road. Yet there still was a chance that it could slide the rest of the way down and maybe into that fast moving stream. The driver's door was solid against a tree and she could see where the car had clipped a few of the trees while it was in the air. She could see that the front end was almost completely destroyed and the reason she had no battery power. Looking at this damage she wondered how she had survived with so little injuries. Standing she noticed that the snow was to her knees and with no knowledge of the surface she carefully headed down the remaining portion of the hill and the headed over to a small grove of trees that she saw. Thinking that there was a good possibility, once she got inside of them, the snow wouldn't be as deep.

The hike to that grove of trees was a struggle and she found that the exercise it required had actually warmed her. The grove turned out to be further than she thought but it provided her two things, privacy, and some protection from the elements. "Privacy, right . . ." she said, and then continued, "As if there is anybody out here that could watch me drop my pants." When she got to that grove of trees she found that it was surrounded by bushes and she had to struggle to work her way through them. This struggle left her breathing a little hard, but was rewarded by a small copse that while it had some snow it was not nearly as deep as what she had hiked through, and completely hid her from any prying eyes. Having never done anything like this she studied the situation for a little while and thought that like in the car leaning against a tree for support she could then take care of the need. "Well, Cath' just do it the longer you stand here the colder you will get, and I suspect our distant ancestors did this without any problem so why am I so hesitant?" She really knew the answer, since as a kid she never liked camping when the family would go do that in the summers. And she really hated those campground bathrooms. So here she was with nothing but the natural world surrounding her.

Once back at the car she thought about the experience, retraced her trip back, and knew she had learned a little. She had touched her bottom once to the snow and that was a shock, but there seemed to be a constant breeze that she continually felt that made her reluctant to perform the necessary function.

Finally successful and feeling better she had struggled back to the car. *What is it about us women anyway? We can talk about our periods, the sex in some of our romance novels, and talk about many, many personal intimate things. We can discuss that incident about our young kids and the messy diapers, but as soon as anybody mentions anything about our normal body functions it is immediately taboo.* Once back inside it appeared to be just as cold inside as out. The skies still looked threatening and as she had approached her wrecked car she looked much closer this time and knew that the only reason it sat where it was, was because of that tree that the driver door rested against. She suspected that if the snow built up on the upper portion of the car and became uneven that it would be enough for the car to finish its slide down the hill and be close to that flowing water, and ice. Still no sounds of activity on the road, and she knew that there was no way to climb back up to the road from here. Eventually she would need to work herself back the way she had come from to find a way back up to the road. One thing for sure she wasn't going to try and cross that fast flowing stream. It just appeared to be too dangerous.

The last thing she wanted to do was spend another night here, but had no idea how to avoid it. She couldn't even remember how far back the last small rural community had been. Besides she was driving and did not know how to convert her driving time to walking time. She did not remember passing any farms or houses in this section of the road. She only remembered seeing the trees, bushes, running water from the many small streams, and not much else. It had always reminded her of some of the fairytales she had grown up with. She could almost imagine Hansel and Gretel approaching her car or maybe Beauty and the Beast with his hidden castle just out of sight. At this moment another verse entered her mind. "Therefore I tell you, do not worry about your life, what you will eat; or about what your body will wear. Life is more than food, and the body more than clothes. Consider the birds; They do not sow or reap, they have no storeroom or barn; yet God feeds them. And how much more valuable you are than the birds." Why did these verses keep coming to her unbidden? Again she then remembered that this one had been in the bathroom next to the mirror. Still at this moment she couldn't see the importance of them. It was just part of home and a part she thought she had avoided. But now it was becoming perfectly clear to her that she hadn't at all.

The waiting seemed to go on forever. There was nothing here but the silence, the whiteness of the snow, the trees, running stream, and the dark gray sullen sky. It just did not look like the storm would be ending soon. Although there had been no new snowfall, it still looked threatening. With little to do time just dragged, but not knowing much about survival in such situations she was at loss as what to do. She had read a little in the book that was with her emergency backpack, but much of it went over her head. It seemed to assume that the reader had some knowledge about such things, which she had to admit she didn't, so things such as deadfalls, drop traps, and desert stills meant nothing to her at all. She thought probably in her case that the Idiots Guide to Survival, if such existed would probably be a better choice. Even there she suspected that she would lack much of the understanding. She was a city kid and proud of it. Leave the country life to those who preferred it. She just wasn't one of them.

Now she wished that she had been more willing to listen to her dad as she was growing up and on those hated family campouts. He seemed to know a lot about the backcountry and what to look for and what to do. She basically ignored it, and after a while her dad had quit trying and passed on what he could to her brother. She thought that what he was trying to teach her would be something she could or would never use – still no activity on that road – just silence. She then came to a decision, that if by midmorning tomorrow, if it wasn't snowing she would leave a note in the car and try and walk out of here. With nothing happening on the road above, while being so close and completely out of reach, she seeming to be the only person alive in this winter wonderland, wherever this was, and in the end it just might come down to it that she would have to rescue herself, experienced or not. After all she would only have to backtrack down the side of the road that was above her until she could find a place that she could then get back on the road. Eventually she would either find a house or maybe that snowplow clearing the road. Right now after having surveyed her car she knew that it was almost invisible. After all, in all honesty, how hard could it be to get back on the road?

Late Saturday Evening – Families

"Where is she?" Keith asked, knowing that no one had an answer. They had called Cathy's parents John and Mary, but they were just as much in the dark as he was. They had told him that she had left right on time and should have been there even with the storm. Now all of them were worried. The route she had taken was one she had taken at least a dozen times. So she should really have known the road. It was just that this new storm had blown in much too quickly from when that last one ended. While late in the season, and storms had arrived in the past this late, this one came out of nowhere. It hadn't even been in the forecast. Yet it had turned out to be a much stronger storm than the one that had just left. "I hope", Keith said, "that wherever she is she's okay." Jan and Jim, Keith's parents looked at each other – both having a worried look, Jim replied saying, "Keith I know this is tough, and that storm just came out of nowhere. All we can do now is hope it is just the storm that has delayed her, and of course get a prayer circle going for her safety."

"You know that's a great idea." Jan said. "I suspect she's alright, but it doesn't hurt getting the Lord involved . . . yes I know she isn't a believer yet, but she comes from a strong Christian home like ours. So I suspect that someday she will understand and see that God and Christ are indeed real and not just some figment of our imagination. Tom, why don't you call the pastor, and I'll get hold of my women's' group. Keith, why don't you call some of your friends on your campus that are members of Christ for Life."

Looking back to his son Tom said, "I also suggest that you continue to try and contact her on her cell phone. I know that the route she takes has some dead areas in it, but at least you can continue to try."

"Oh believe me, I have been, and will continue to."

They sprang into action with Jim calling the pastor, Jan making contact with the leader of the women's group and Keith trying to get in contact with the Youth pastor at the college. Jan followed up by making a call back to Cathy's family and found that they had been doing the very same thing. In a short time much prayer would be going out to Jesus for the safe return of Cathy. While the very same actions were taking place with Cathy's parents, they contacting their church, and putting out the call for prayer for the safe return of their daughter. "Where could she be?" Mary asked.

Taking his wife in his arms, all John could do was shake his head and say, "I really don't know, I really just don't know, and I wish I could give you a truthful answer . . . but . . . yeah I know. If wishes were money we would have been wealthy people." Then holding his wife he felt helpless as to what to do, or what direction to turn. Prayer seemed to be the only thing available to them at this moment. There was just too much distance to cover and she could be anywhere along that route. At least she hadn't removed that emergency backpack he had put together even though he could tell that she hadn't wanted anything to do with it. It showed in every fiber of her body, but he could tell she would do it just to humor him. Now it could mean the difference between her living and her dying. And with her not knowing the Savior it was not something he really wanted to see happen. At this point he picked up the Bible and started reading his favorite passages, the promises given, and also the power of prayer. He needed to get word out to one of the national Christian organizations so their daughter could be put on the national prayer chain. Yes there would be much prayer going out to heaven this day.

Sunday Afternoon – Cathy

The storm seemed to continue to hold off, but the sky held no promises. It was still dark, gray, and formless, with the feel of impending snow. Once again the winds had picked up and were bitterly cold. If she stepped out of her car for a moment the winds would immediately chill her to the bone. While it wasn't much warmer in the wreck, at least it was out of that wind. If the winds had emotion they appeared to be angry. While it wasn't snowing at this time it might as well have been. As the winds were blowing they were picking up the freshly fallen stuff shifting and piling it everywhere. Because of the amount of snow the winds were blowing around it was almost impossible to see where one was going. It had to be below zero out there with the wind chill alone. With her body heat and the moisture in the air every window was frosted over and when she wiped some of it off she could see ice forming. It was just nasty out there right now. The day had been slow, cold, and boring, and seemed to just drag. With the darkness of the cloud cover it was almost impossible to even guess the time of day. She hadn't worn a watch in a few years. It seemed that her body was one that would kill watches in a few months so she gave up on them — Instead, depending on the clocks in the house, and of course in her car, and now and then on the radio. Although she considered radio a wasteland, and only would listen when she either got tired or her personal selection of tunes or when there was something she needed to listen for.

A number of times she thought that maybe it was getting close to evening because of the darkening of the sky only to have it brighten again as the cloud cover thickened and thinned. She had always considered herself a pretty good tracker of time, but now realized it was because of routine not because she could. Now she worried because of the strength of the wind could she hear anyone or anything coming down that road? Again with her windows frosted and beginning to freeze she just couldn't watch for anyone. Besides this was the fact that the upper side of her car was buried in snow, so the only way to watch for anything was to leave the confines of her car, and at this moment this was the last thing she wanted to do. Damn, she was cold. She couldn't remember ever being this cold, and there was no place to get warm. She now dreamed of the heat of summer and how, at times, she would complain about it being much too hot. Right this minute she would take much too hot that was for sure. She was surrounded by a white cold wasteland with temperatures dangerously cold, and time for her could be running out much too soon.

She knew that she was losing heat through those windows but had no way to cover them. Still she knew that until the winds stopped she couldn't leave the confines of her car. She did not think that she would last more than 30 minutes in that freezing wind. It was strong enough that even though the car was against a large tree, both the tree and the car shook. She could actually feel the tree sway in the winds. She hoped it would not be enough to shake the car loose and have it continue its slide down the embankment, followed by possibly entering into that fast moving stream. Now she kicked herself for not remembering that book that she had left on her nightstand. She had wanted to bring it but was in such a hurry to get out the door and on the road that she left it there. Chills ran up and down her spine from being so cold and her hands were almost numb. She sat on them and at the same time felt the heat from her body and the cold from her hands. Her feet were as cold. She then remembered that someone had told her if her hands and feet were cold to put on a hat – whether there was any truth to that statement she didn't really know. She didn't have a hat, but remembered that she did bring some towels and then took them out. Thinking about it she said very softly, "Hmmm, I only have a few with me . . . I bet if I put this big one inside my clothes and wrap it around me like when I get out of the shower that it will be another layer to help. Then I'll use the . . . ah . . . wet hair towel to wrap up my head . . . Hey I bet I can use some socks for my hands. Probably will look ridiculous, but I don't care."

She had driving gloves that allowed the fingers to be bare but had left her heavy gloves with her ski equipment. Had she thrown that bag in her trunk she would even have had a heavy jacket. But all that was back home and sitting uselessly in her closet. All she could do at this moment was shake her head and curse herself for her stupidity. Yes, she had driven this road without incident so many times that she just took it for granted, and so had become careless in her preparation. Now once again she realized that her carelessness could kill her. "No!" She screamed, "I am going to survive this!" Then as the emotion built up inside of her again she began to cry, "Oh God, why me, why now? Why when so much of my life is ahead of me?" At this moment another scripture entered into her mind. "Have I not commanded you? Be strong and courageous. Do not be terrified; do not be discouraged, for the Lord your God will be with you wherever you go." Joshua 1:9. "Did I memorize every plaque in our house? And where is this one located?" She asked herself. Thinking about it she then remembered that this one was located on the wall between the kitchen and the living room. So you had to pass it every time you went into the kitchen. And it was a path she had taken she suspected thousands of times. Shaking her head she thought, *So am I going to end up remembering every one of those many . . . oh I don't know how many . . . plaques that mother was so fond of?*

Suddenly she realized that even at Keith's home she couldn't get away from those plaques. As Keith's mother seemed almost as fond of them as her own mother. She remembered that over the door leading out of the house was the one that said, "As for me and my house we will serve the Lord." Joshua 24:15. Then thinking about it she realized that they were everywhere there too, not quite a numerous, but there just the same. She found that even though consciously she had tried to avoid them, her subconscious had seen and read them anyway. What was it anyway? Couldn't she just get those sayings out of her mind? After all she still considered herself above all that first century thinking.

Very Late Saturday – Very Early Sunday to Sunday Afternoon - Families

"I think it time we called the Highway Patrol." Mary stated, "I just got off the phone with Keith and his parents and there still hasn't been a sign or a call from her. I am very worried that something really bad has happened to her, and yes I know that there is a good chance that once this is over she will be safe. Then all this worrying that we are doing will be just that. But you know as I do that this silence is not like her. Even though she seems to have fought us at every turn she still would obey and would always check in."

"Very true . . . she did always put up a fight, but in the end would do as she should. Yeah I agree if truth be told, I had really just come to the same conclusion anyway. And again like you just stated she probably is safe and just waiting out the storm somewhere and unable to contact anyone. Still at this point I think I at least want to get the word out. After all, if she is in serious trouble I would never be able to forgive myself if I just let it lay."

Mary waited patiently while her husband John went to contact the authorities. While waiting her mind drifted a little, this brought a smile to her. She and her husband had such ordinary names, and in the end they had kept it the same for their children. She could remember the games the two of them would play with their names, as in the old "B" romances, their names had been used a lot. Her thoughts were interrupted as John returned and he had a real worried look on his face. "What's wrong dear?" She asked

Shaking his head he hesitated a moment then said, "The information I got from them wasn't good. When I put in the information that our daughter was missing and the route she had taken, what I got back wasn't promising. The dispatcher said that the surprise second storm has left many stranded, and the snowplows are unable to keep up with the double whammy. So only the main roads are being worked and opened. The route she took is little traveled and it will probably be a week before the plows can even find time to clear that road. Then she asked if we had heard anything at all from her, and of course I told her no. I also explained that we knew that there were a number of areas on the road where there was no signal for the cell phones. Something to do with the mountains and trees I suspect."

"So did they say they were going to be able to do anything?"

"She said that they would be on the lookout for her, but that presently they were completely overwhelmed. She also said that she would inform the dispatchers of the county Sheriff so that their local patrols could be watching for her. So other than that, it was the best they could do for now. I guess, as if you didn't know, it truly is in the hands of our Lord."

Wringing her hands and looking up into John's eyes she could see the worry there, and she assumed that hers were no different. They came together and hugged each other deeply fearing the worst and hoping for the best. Their child was probably in very serious trouble and might even at this moment be fighting for her life and they were helpless. "I guess we have to have faith", John whispered, "since this is beyond us and only God knows the outcome and direction this will take."

Putting her head in his chest, all she could do was nod in agreement. Here they were safe and warm and Cathy could be dying and she felt so very lost. She could feel the emotions starting build inside of her again. Knowing at this moment if she tried to speak she would cry, she remained silent taking the strength from her husband. She knew that even though he wouldn't say it he probably was just as lost. So she suspected that he probably was holding her for her strength, and they together were looking towards God for his. "I think we need to take out the Bible read some scripture, and then pray about this again. And to leave it God's hands, knowing that even in this he has a purpose." Then separating from his wife he went and retrieved the much used Bible and the two then went to the kitchen table, and then started reading in Luke, Jesus's words looking for comfort. Then hand in hand they prayed for Cathy's safe return, knowing that prayer for the safe return of their daughter was going out to God in many places.

* * *

Keith, pacing the floor in the foyer, was at a complete loss as to what to do. Cathy, his bride to be, was out there somewhere and with this storm there was absolutely nothing he could do to help. He had begun to look to himself as partly her protector from things that could take one down in life, but already it was becoming apparent that it was going to be much more complicated than he ever imagined. He felt completely helpless, lost, and it frustrated him to no end.

"Son, I really understand how you are feeling at this moment. And I really do know the helplessness when you really want to do something but have no direction to even start. I suspect that God may have his hand in this and whatever the outcome we must trust in him."

"Yeah, I know dad . . . it's just so hard. The woman I love is out there somewhere and I suspect in real trouble and here I am safe and warm and unable to do anything. At first I thought, just go out and look, but with the storm as strong as it is I suspect, in the end, that instead of just me trying to find Cathy it would have ended with both of us lost . . . not a good thing at all. So here I am . . . well here I am and not knowing, is tough!"

"Believe me in this, I really do know how you are feeling at this moment. First before I tell you how let me say that there will be an important lesson for all of us that will come out of this."

"Important lesson? I don't understand that at all."

Putting his arms around his son's shoulders he continued, "Okay Keith let's go sit in the living room then I will try to explain it as I see it." Steering him in that direction Jim turned to his wife and asked, "Jan can you bring us some coffee into the living room, and then join us there please?" He sat on the couch so that Jan could join him. He had Keith sit across from him on the recliner and commented saying, "Just relax for a couple and when your mother has brought the coffee . . . in fact I think it's only right that I help, and then we will continue to talk." He got back up and went out to the kitchen to assist Jan with the coffee, giving himself a little more time to think about what he wanted to say.

Jan, seeing him approach said, "Thanks, I know this is a very tough time for Keith, and I know it's not any easier for us or Cathy's parents, but what can we do? I mean really, what can we do?"

Shaking his head he said, "In truth just about what we are doing right now. Until this weather breaks there is little chance of going out there and trying to find her. My gosh, if you think about it, there's around five hundred miles of road alone, but I think we can narrow it down quite a bit. But before I say any more I want to have Keith in this conversation. I'll take Keith's and my cup out and you can bring yours and maybe some of those cookies to go with the coffee. See you out there shortly." He picked up the two cups of coffee and returned to the living room where Keith was still sitting, but he was sitting on the edge of the chair leaning forward as he took the coffee from his dad. Keith said, "Thanks, I couldn't but overhear what you and mom was talking about what is happening, and I guess you are as worried as I am. I suspected it would be that way, but I really never truly knew. I know that when the two of us started dating that you and mom admonished me about her disbelief of God and Christ. But all I can say is it just seemed right, right from the beginning and has only grown stronger leading me to eventually propose to her asking her to be my wife. I didn't take it lightly then and knowing the responsibility that this leads to, I continue to think about it even now."

Jan came in from the kitchen at that moment and sat down next to her husband and set the cookies down between them on the table that sat there, and said, "Yes, we knew that it was serious almost from the beginning. The worry we had was that her disbelief could lead you away from God. If that had happened it wouldn't have been the first time such a thing has happened, and I suspect not the last. But you held on to your beliefs all the way through." At this point Jan leaned forward and looked into her son's eyes. "For that we are very proud of you, and for your commitment to this girl, we truly couldn't be happier. She seems to be just as serious about you. I guess if we had ever doubted this then her trip coming here, this one that she hasn't completed as of yet, is the proof."

"That's probably true mom, but it's of little consequence at this moment since she wasn't able to complete the journey and now is missing. Frankly it flat out scares me to my very soul. I mean after finding someone, someone who I think may be my soul mate, and then to possibly lose her . . ." At this point the emotion choked his words off before he could continue. He took a deep breath and continued, "Just as we were getting ready to become one under God's kingdom and then start our growth as husband

and wife . . . I mean to lose that even before we had a chance is almost too hard to bear."

There was silence for a short period of time then Jim said, "I will tell you this son, I do know what you are going through."

"I know", Keith asked, "you and mom are very strong in your relationship with each other and it's obvious that you two love each other, but how can you know this?"

"Okay, now before I explain that one and your mother will tell you some things too, I want you to understand why I feel that God has his hand in this. First Cathy needs to see for herself what God can do. And I suspect she is finding much out about herself right at this time, whatever the outcome may be. Secondly, for her family members and us, it forces us to put our faith where it belongs and to test us to see if we are indeed as strong in the faith as we should be. To be honest, as you well know, we are helpless to do anything about this situation, and we can either get angry about it or turn to the only one who can do something about it. Does that make sense to you?"

"Yeah, I guess I can kind of see that, but sure isn't easy."

"Easy isn't allowed in these words that were just spoken. And marriage is the toughest thing you will ever do." She smiled to soften the words she had just spoken before continuing. "As you know your dad has worked in a number of different jobs over the years.

Early in our marriage he worked for the state park system and helped put out those wildfires. While none of them were ever large, the fires always scared me, and I would worry all the time when your dad would not show up at home when he was supposed to. Then I would find out that he was out on some fireline somewhere, which would make me worry that much more. But I was helpless, I couldn't be there and there was never any information. And sometimes some rumor would get started that someone was either hurt or killed. So I would try to spend my time taking care of you and your younger brother, both of you were very young then, and pray, and try and keep my mind off of what he was doing. If he didn't return soon, then I would have to cart the two of you off to your grandparent's house, as I had to work then to keep us afloat. But even when I would be at work, I would be distracted and just couldn't get it out of my head the danger that your dad could be in. I mean it was something that could have killed him, and this could have left me a widow and with two small children to boot. And the thought of losing him, well, I have to admit that it scared me to death."

Reaching for a cookie and then munching on it Jim picked up the conversation from Jan's comment, "I knew that it was something that really bothered your mother." He paused for a moment looking over at his wife with loving eyes before continuing. "But at the same time it was something I really loved doing. Yet, every day that I would leave I could see the fear in her eyes and it was tearing me apart inside. Eventually things changed and I moved up and out of the fire-fighting end and became a full time employee working in the recreation section. As you know as time went on I became the head ranger of the district, which is where I am right now. And if things go right in a few more years I will be able to retire and give more time to your mother here, and she really deserves it."

Blushing a little Jan then asked, "Now Jim, how do you mean that?"

Smiling back at his wife he responded, "Anyway you want to take it honey . . . any way that works for you."

Smiling Keith thought, *this is something I have always loved about my parents. It is just so obvious that my dad loves everything about my mom and she the same about my dad. I can only hope that Cathy and I can be as close and as loving.* Then he realized that it was early Sunday morning and tomorrow would be Monday and since he presently was home from college he would be the only one home. That meant that he was going to have to be the one who would keep the two families informed of any updates that might come in. He knew that his dad had hated it when Jan had to go back to work. But unfortunately it was something they both knew that there had been no choice. So his mother worked as a receptionist at a local dentist office, and had her schedule set up that she could be home when they would get home from school those so many years ago.

Of course both he and his brother were long past that time in their lives. He was just finishing college and his brother in his second year. But even still his mother had continued at that dentist office, even though it was just part time – more to assist, since she had been there around twenty years and knew all the patients and exactly how the office ran. He knew that she would keep at it until her husband, his father would retire and then she would then too. They lived on his salary presently and put all of her income away for their future. It had allowed them to live debt free for many years now, and he hoped that somehow he could do the same when he and Cathy were married. This last thought gave him pause. Since, right at this moment, he did not know where she was and if she was even alive. Still he felt that if she wasn't alive that somehow he would know. And at this moment he felt that she was still alive, but other than that he knew nothing. He then realized that his dad was talking.

" . . . It's something you learn over the years, that there are certain things that each of you does that is consistent."

"Sorry dad, I was thinking about something else briefly and didn't quite hear what you said."

Smiling Jim said, "Thinking about Cathy I suspect. What I was trying to say is that in a relationship you learn that there are things that each of you do that are consistent, and it is that stuff that becomes the normal and routine, it is what makes us who we are. We become comfortable with these small things and know after a time that this is the way it will work. At this point one takes much for granted and it is easy to relax within this relationship. But when something happens that is out of character it is then you find out where your relationship truly stands. I don't mean this in a negative way at all. Ah, let me give you an example that happened with us, and then I think you will understand. Are with me so far?"

"Yes dad, go ahead."

"One of the things that your mother liked to do a couple of times a month was to go and visit her parents, your grandparents. Most of the time I would stay home, as there was plenty of stuff that needed to be done here to keep me more than busy. Anyway before coming back home she would call let me know that you all were on the way back home. At this point I knew that within an hour she would be pulling back into the driveway and she and the two of you would be safe. This one time I got the call and Jan I know you remember the incident . . ." Jan smiled and nodded yes. He then continued. " . . . I expected her home and she didn't show up. At this point I thought that she just got hung up at her parent's house and it just made her a little late. But as time continued to pass and she still made no appearance I became worried and then alarmed. What had happened, where was she? I called and her parents said that she had left right after the phone call, and this is before cell phones, so that even worried me more. Again, what had happened to her and of course the two of you? This was not how she was, and of course my thoughts were towards the worst. No word or anything, and no idea where to even look, what can you do? It's kind of like what's happening now with Cathy. You know that this is not like her at all and so you can only worry since you really cannot do anything yourself. It is at times like this you find out just how much you love and need that other person. It is times like this that really makes one appreciate what you have. In the end she had broken down just around the corner from her parents and was eventually able to get the car running again and then come on home. But I have to admit that during her absence I was very worried, and felt completely helpless, and of course as now, I turned to God, and asked for her safe return. I really do not know why we are built the way we are but, it seems that it takes something like this for us to really understand our feelings."

"Yeah, I can see that as I am kind of in that situation right now and you are right it is really showing me just how much I care."

His mother smiled adding, "Yes I remember that incident all too well, and it was very frustrating for me. I had two young boys in the car who were fidgeting, and a car that just quit. It would start then quit. So I figured that if I just let it sit a while that it would finally start up again." Then looking over at her husband before looking back at Keith she continued. "Your dad always tried to make sure the cars I drove wouldn't break down, but this one just decided that it would. While I was in a familiar neighborhood, I really wasn't close to anyone I knew. I figured that eventually this car would start, and eventually it did, and I got back home safely. And of course when I got home your dad heard all about it."

Laughing a little Keith said, "Yeah I bet and in more ways than one."

They all laughed at that one because it was true. The conversation continued for a while longer and then they just drifted off all lost in their own thoughts. Keith had turned around and was just staring out the window allowing his mind to go wherever it decided at the moment. He was at a complete loss as to what to do other than pray. All of them had been doing that once they felt something had been wrong. The skies were still dark and sullen with the promise of more snow, but so far that promise had held off. *Where is she?* It would soon be dark and he knew that it would be getting colder. *Could she survive this night and possibly others in this weather?* At this point he just got up and started pacing unsure of anything. Wanting to do something positive but knew that if he went out in this threatening weather that he could complicate things and become lost and a victim of the storm also. So waiting was all that he could do, and he was finding it to be one of the toughest things he had ever done.

He felt an arm on his shoulder and turned and saw his dad standing there. He could see the concern in his eyes as the stood a faced each other. "Keith, waiting and not knowing is one of the hardest things you will ever do, as if you haven't figured that out. Because we are kind of the 'let's go and fix it' type guys we want to do just that. So when God puts us in a situation that leaves us helpless, like this one, it makes us think the worst. We wonder why can we not get out there and do something. I am sure you have thought that way. I know through the years when something came up that put me in this type of situation it is the way I reacted, and I can see it's the same for you. We men like to think we can protect those that we love, and to fix the problems that they face, or maybe lessen them. Yet there are many things we will never be able to lessen for our women. At those times all we can do is support them as best as we can, and let God do his work. A good example of that is childbirth. It is the two of you that created that child, but it is her burden to have it grow inside of her and then bring it into the world. During that birthing time you can see the work and pain she goes through and there is nothing you can do to make it easier, or stop the pain. All you can do is be there and support her throughout those difficult times. Yet when it is over you feel an even stronger love bond that flows between the two of you.

I guess what I am trying to say is that probably if we really looked at things we would find that much of the protection that we think we provide is probably an illusion anyway. I mean we really try. Yet our loved ones go out on their own almost everyday and we aren't there at those times. So we must trust that God is there for them, and he is. But at times we begin to take things for granted and do not really appreciate what we have. As I said earlier it is these times that the truth is shown to us."

"Yes, I can see that dad. I am finding out quickly that I care more deeply for Cathy than I thought I did. Just where is she, and . . . what can I do? I know the answer for now, but it doesn't make it any easier, or for me to have the patience to just wait this out. Yeah I know, but what else can you do?"

Shaking his head knowing exactly what his son was going through he said, "Not much more than what we are doing now. Once things finally break then we may finally be able to do something, but until then, here we are." He turned to leave and Keith said, "Thanks dad. I think I am beginning to understand more about you and mom now that I am entering a very serious relationship with Cathy. I think it does really take one to be in something similar to learn about what you have observed over your life." At this point they separated and went their own ways leaving Keith again alone with his thoughts, staring once again out the window at the dark countryside as night arrived and slowly worked its way towards the morning light.

Late Sunday Afternoon / Early Evening – Cathy

It was getting colder and the winds were picking up again. With the sky threatening to release snow once more. All of her windows now were completely iced over and ice crystals were forming in her water. She was now wearing everything she had brought with her. While it helped, she was uncomfortable from the tightness of the many layers and still cold. Now for sure she knew that night was approaching, but now became very worried about the increasing cold. Could she make it through another night? Again another plaque entered her mind. "Forever God is Faithful, Forever God is Strong, Forever God is with us, Forever!" *Chris Tomlin paraphrase Psalm 136.* Well, at least this one wasn't directly from the Bible, but still had made a statement about this first century god. Why did so may still believe in him? And where was this plaque located? She thought about it and then remembered that it was in the dining room on the wall among the many family pictures that were there. Oh to be there now where it was so nice and warm with the smells wafting out of the kitchen leaving one anticipating the good meal that would be there soon. Would she ever see it again?

Sunday Afternoon – Families

Both families had returned from church earlier on Sunday, and both had asked the members of their respective congregations to pray for the safe return of Cathy. With Cathy's family there was much support, and they knew that the sermon the pastor had given was a good one, but being as distracted as they were really didn't remember much of it at all. After returning in the early afternoon, they could tell that it was getting colder which only made them worry more. "Where is she?" Mary asked. "I hope she is all right. This not knowing is just killing me."

John seeing his wife could read the fear and worry in her eyes and her body could only shake his head. He had no answers, no solutions, and knew that it truly was in God's hands. He then stated, "Mary I wish there were some answers to those questions you just asked. What I wouldn't give to know those answers myself. I guess I could lie, to you and myself, and say she is safe and is just waiting until the roads are cleared before she continues her travels, but even I can't believe that. She's out there somewhere probably fighting for her life, and no I won't say it, I think we both would know if it was the worst. Unfortunately it appears that soon this second storm is going to start snowing again, and this will make it even more difficult. All we can do is what we are supposed to do and that is put it into God's hands. Many times we think, even in our faith that we can accomplish things without his help, but I really think it's all an illusion. I mean that even when we think we are doing something without his help that it is there in the background guiding our steps anyway."

Looking up into her husband's eyes Mary said, "I know you are right, but this is so hard, not knowing, not being able to do anything, and not being there to help her in her need. I feel the need to reach out and hug her and keep her close. And I can't do any of that. This is just tearing me up. I feel so helpless, and as her mother it makes it almost impossible for me to think of anything else."

"Tell you what I'll call Keith's parents, Jim and Jan, shortly. I know they have a little further to travel after the service to get home. I am sure that Keith probably stayed home so that there would be someone there just in case. But I think he has enough to worry about. I am sure that like us he wants to get out and help find her, but knows that by trying to do something like that in this storm could only put him in danger and that would do nothing but harm. Why don't you go ask John Jr. if there have been any calls while we were out. I told him to stay home today so that he could monitor our phones here. I'll get us some coffee going, and then we could put together a quick lunch. How does that sound?"

"Okay John, I'll go talk to our son, and I think I would prefer some herbal tea instead. Maybe some coffee later this afternoon, I need that tea right now to relax me. I'm just so wound up inside, and really scared."

Holding her close they both stood in silence, then she turned and went upstairs to where their son was with John heading into the kitchen to get some water going for her tea, and putting on a small pot of coffee for himself. *Where is she?* He thought once again. Then thinking about it he decided to get out a map of her route and try and do some studying to see what he could eliminate. It still might be a day or two before this present storm broke, but once it did, and once the roads were open again he and the rest of the family would want to have the area to be searched as small as possible.

Shortly Mary returned and he could see before she said anything that there had been nothing new to add, no phone calls, and no news. When she saw him watching her all she could do was shake her head no. "Nothing new to add . . . Other than a couple of calls from friends there have been just nothing."

He thought a moment, smiled encouragingly and said, "I guess I can understand that. Like you I would like to know something, anything, but I guess nothing can be considered good news too. I mean they could be calling us and telling us the worst possible news, and right now it's one I wouldn't really want to get.

So I guess I will have to consider the silence as a sign that at least there's still a chance she is alive."

The afternoon seemed like it was lasting forever, and again other than calls of support from friends the phones were silent. John had taken out a map and had spread it out on the kitchen table and was attempting to narrow down the area to look for her when the weather finally did break and the roads became passable again. "Mary, what time did she leave Saturday, do you remember?"

"It wasn't as early as I had expected her to leave, since she seemed really eager to see Keith, but I think it was around nine or ten in the morning."

"Which one . . . nine or ten? It could make a big difference. I was outside in the shop until around 11:30, so I didn't even hear her leave. She may have even looked in on me before she left, but if she did I didn't see her."

"I think I did glance up at the clock when she said that she was leaving. I was on the phone at the time with mom, and remember saying to be safe and to call us when she arrived." She then paused for a couple of minutes as she tried to remember, and then said, "It was 9:15, I am almost sure of it."

"Okay, if I remember right this new storm rolled in pretty fast, completely unexpected and the temperatures began to fall quickly. I think that it began to snow again, at least when I noticed it around 3:00 in the afternoon. With its quick arrival it started to get nasty right away. So she would have been on the road around five and half-hours. I think she probably would have stopped for lunch, which means that driving time would be closer 4 and half-hours. That's giving her an hour to eat, and then be on the road again. So guessing she was probably averaging about 50 miles in an hour, since much of what she was traveling was backcountry roads that would place her somewhere in the range of 200 to 225 miles into her trip. Do you remember the name of that little roadside diner she said that she always stopped at when she drove over there?"

"Not immediately, why is that important?" Mary asked.

"I want to call it and see if they remember her being there. If they do then we will know that she got at least that far and can guess how much farther she got before the weather became a factor. Also call Keith and his family and let them know when she left. I am sure that they are doing the same thing, trying to figure out where she might be so any information we can give them will help also. I am sure once we are able to travel the roads again that they will start from their end and we from ours, giving us better coverage – especially if we can narrow it down. My guess is she would have been close to half way there, especially if we can get it confirmed she had stopped at that diner."

"John, that's an excellent idea! Okay just let me think a moment, hmmm, wasn't it something like 'stop here' or 'come on in' or something like that?"

"That's right, it really was an unusual name, and it was located just about right for people to want to take a break from their driving, no matter which direction that they may be coming from. It was in, oh what would you guess, maybe a gas station, a store which I think also had a feed store attached, and maybe a hardware store and the post office . . . So – including the diner – no more than five or six buildings there by the road." He paused as he thought about it and said, "Wasn't it *Take a Break Café*?"

Excited Mary exclaimed, "I think that's exactly right and wasn't the little town called *Hillstown*?"

"Yes, I know that when we have traveled that route, which of course has been much less than she has, I remembered that there seemed to be many small towns throughout that area. But then there is that one stretch where probably for a hundred miles there seems to be nothing, just the two-lane blacktop winding through the mountains. I always thought it was a beautiful area, and I think if I remember right its national forest, probably one of the reasons that there's nothing around. Okay, I know that the dispatcher that I talked to said she would contact the county sheriff but I'll see if I can call the one locally there in Hillstown, and also try and call that café and see if anyone is there. I suspect with this weather that most likely there will be no one at the café since this second storm has locked down the roads."

Sunday Night – Cathy

It was cold and getting colder, and she was beginning to wonder if she would survive the night. Dusk was approaching and the winds had picked up again. She had to use the cup only once this day, and never had the urge to take another trip to that copse, for which she was very thankful. Once was enough! It had humbled her, a little, to realize that something that was so natural was so difficult. Another fear entered her mind as she had opened the back seat again to place the filled cup back into the trunk; it was beginning to snow again. Could she survive another very cold night in the car? Well one thing for sure, she wouldn't be able to survive outside. Again how did the animals do it? She then remembered that in the survival handbook there was a chapter on surviving in the cold in your car. Eagerly she dug into the side pouch of the backpack, found the book, and then immediately dropped it. Her hands were numb and she could barely feel anything. Her feet hurt and she knew that she was in desperate trouble. Picking up the paperback she opened it and found that it was now too dark to be able to read it. She then dug out the flashlight, and used it to set up a candle, which she lit.

While the flickering light from the candle was dim, she found that she could make out the words on the pages. One of the first things it mentioned was that usually one in this type of situation one doesn't think about what would be available to help, and at the same time, reluctant to do any further damage to their car. Never realizing that most likely that the car would be a total loss anyway, and any further damage they would do would not change that fact at all. It went on to say that survival is what it is all about. Why *be* a body in a pretty interior, instead be someone who is alive in a destroyed interior. One of the first suggestions was not to build a fire inside your car. Too many items gave off poisonous gases, and carbon monoxide could also build up. Both could and would kill. Instead use the interior to add layers to one's clothing – cut or tear off the material that covers the seats, and add that to what one was wearing.

As she was reading this her teeth were chattering and knew that most likely if she was like this now what would she be like in a couple of hours once what little heat from the sun had completely dissipated. Again digging into the backpack she found the sheathed hunting knife that was part of the emergency kit and carefully reached over the two front seats, then slowly cut the seat back materials and carefully worked them off the frame. As she struggled to pull it off the frames she found that the material got stuck on the top where the headrest entered into the frame. She found that she again had to use the knife to finally get the material to release from the frames. The effort left her breathing hard and there were clouds forming from her breath, before the cold made them vanish. Finally successful she held up the material and saw that it had a foam lining. "Something to help insulate me", she said to herself. "Looks like I'll need to make some slits so that my arms can fit through the sides, but with the hole I cut through the top won't need to worry about a hole for my head."

Once she completed her cutting she worked herself into the seating material. Initially it was cold, but slowly she could feel some warmth as her body warmed the material. The foam was acting as insulation and she could see that it was helping to hold the cold out. Not quite sure how to treat the second one she temporarily put her legs in it as the first one only covered her to her waist. This was followed by thinking, *I guess if it becomes necessary I can remove the other portion from the front seats and find a way to use that material too.* At this point she took another inventory of her dwindling supplies, and was quite happy that her dad had put the MRE's in the emergency kit. They would self-heat, and anything warm was welcome. But what she was finding out was that as she would take a spoon or fork full of the food that by the time she put it in her mouth it had almost become cold – a sure sign that it had to be close to zero. She found that the water in the water bottles was also beginning to freeze. So to have anything to drink she had to keep a bottle close to her – Not a problem really, as ice water didn't appeal to her right now anyway. Could she or would she survive another night? One thing for sure, she felt at this moment with her lack of experience that she had done everything she knew how to do.

The only other thing she could do is pray. "There! I thought it", she exclaimed. But then again if there really was a God why would he care about her? After all this deity would have created the whole universe, and she knew for a fact that she lived on a minor planet with a minor common ordinary star keeping them alive, in the vast suburbs of the milky way galaxy. And this galaxy was just one of probably billions. So with something so vast why would such a deity care at all? Yet that was exactly what the Bible said. She had heard it all of her life, at least until she became an adult and went to college. Yes she was still living at home, but she had plans for that to end. Marriage to Keith was something she had been anticipating and now she just did not know, just really did not know what was going to happen to her. Again, would she survive the night? Thinking for a little while she finally whispered, "God, if you are real, please help. I have so much of my life ahead of me and want to live it, but now I have placed myself in this very dangerous position, and I just don't know of any way out. Can you hear me? Mom and dad say that you hear every prayer that goes out to you, even from unbelievers like me." Whispering the words she found that she could feel the emotions and depression beginning to build.

She had felt better about praying, but still didn't feel that it had gone anywhere. But it at least allowed her to put into words some of her present fears. Again these thoughts started the tears flowing, since it appeared to be hopeless with no way out. She was scared to her very core. She feared that even though she had survived the initial accident that she would die from, what is it called, oh yes, exposure. She had heard of such things happening all the time and had wondered what these people may have been thinking as they neared death and knew that they were going to die. Now she was afraid that she was about to find out for herself. She, sitting on the back seat leaned against the downhill door, and pulled her legs up to her with her arms around them and once again cried it out.

Hillstown Local County Sheriff

The dispatcher had alerted him and the rest of the county sheriffs in this area to look for a missing vehicle. The suspicion was that it probably was involved in a single vehicle TC (Traffic Collision). The person driving the vehicle had never reached her destination, and this backcountry road was the one she traveled. He, for one, felt that if she had left the road, and with the amount of snow that had fallen and what was still threatening that there would be little chance of finding her, oh, probably until spring. It wouldn't be the first time such had happened, and he knew sadly that it would not be the last. The present storm had come out of nowhere and had hit hard, and appeared that it was refusing to give up. He expected more snow from it tonight. He was the resident sheriff for this small town, and right now, even with his four-wheel drive vehicle and chains, it was almost impossible to get around. He had to be very careful. Again he knew that it probably would be days before the snowplows would be able to get to them and free up the roads. There just wasn't enough traffic to warrant it at this time. So normally they were one of the last areas to be cleared.

He thought that he would travel down to the café and see if anyone there might have remembered seeing the woman. For such a small place that café had always been busy with travelers. The cafe seemed to be located in just about the right spot for travelers wanting to take a break from their driving. He had a description of the car and the family had sent a photo over the Internet to the law enforcement closest to them, who then forwarded it out to the county sheriff department. So armed with the photo and such he was out being careful so as to not end up as a victim of the weather himself. He had to admit that from the photo the young woman was not beautiful, but pretty at least. He could see his own daughter, who was younger than this woman, staring out at him from this picture.

As he was carefully driving the roads he thought about how long he had been the resident sheriff here in this small community of Hillstown. Shaking his head he realized that he and his wife had been here eleven years. "Just where has the time gone." He said to himself. Then he laughed. How many times had he heard others say the very same thing? *One thing for sure time waits on no one, and it just seems to speed by. And, before you know it years have passed.* While on this train of thought he began to think about the families and of the different individuals who lived here and their different personalities. It was something that was critical in his line of work. With that knowledge he could approach a situation knowing something about who was involved and what and how they might react. This immediately brought to his mind one of the long time locals who is a writer. They had sat and talked a number of times over the years at the café, and he considered him somewhat eccentric. After all, who would lock himself up all winter in an isolated cabin with no way out except on foot or snowmobile? The cabin had no power, no phone, no commercial radio, nothing. It was very primitive living that was for sure. When he had asked him why he did this every winter, Will said, "I find that for me to be successful that I have to have no distractions at all. During the rest of the year

I am coming up with ideas, finding sources for my articles, and promoting my books. There is very little time for me to concentrate. And all these conveniences that the modern world provides are just distractions taking me away from what I need to do. So in the winter by staying there, and knowing there is no way to leave or even hear what is happening in the outside world I can concentrate on my writing. It works for me, and has for many years. So I guess until something changes in me I'll just continue working that way. Yep, just me and my dog spend the winter there and believe it or not it actually goes by pretty fast."

Winter would be coming to an end soon, so he expected to see Will Fellows shortly. With a full beard and probably hair down to his shoulders since he didn't cut it himself, and he kept a beard to keep his face warm in all of that snow. Shortly after returning to civilization the beard would be gone and he would have had his hair cut, no longer looking like the mountain man from the 1800's. At first when he had arrived he had worried about this guy living like that through the winter months, but none of the other town members seemed too worried. They had passed on to him that Will had been doing this for years, and probably would be doing this long after he wasn't the resident sheriff around Hillstown anymore. A bump in the road, and the four wheel drive slipping, brought him back to reality and for a moment he had to fight for control. With some fast maneuvering he was successful in keeping it on the road. He had chains on, and of course was traveling slowly, but even with them it was obvious that there was ice under that snow. He knew that after this visit to the café that he needed to check in on a couple of the residents here. There was a single mother struggling to keep things afloat just outside of town. Her husband had been a marine and was killed in action somewhere in the Middle East – unfortunately something that seemed to happen much too much. He knew the necessity of it but that didn't make it any easier on the families when they lost a loved one. This one never even got a chance to hold their most recent child. And, of course, as in any community, there were always the local troublemakers. Some from just having nothing to do, others just were bad. But overall the town was quiet.

He had called ahead to make sure the cafe was open, and found that the owner, cook, and one waitress were there. Laughing the owner said that for some reason things were quite slow, but a couple of the locals had showed up. She figured that for the next few days she would only keep it open to late afternoon and until the roads were cleared only the locals, and very few of them would be showing up. Well he was still at least twenty minutes from arriving because of the conditions, but it's better to be safe than sorry. Now paying closer attention to the road and his driving, he then informed the dispatcher of the road conditions and his destination. He then told her that as soon as he had any information to add to the missing person case that he would let her know immediately. Again, while the repeaters were good for the official stuff, things like fire, law enforcement, and road crews, the cell towers were spotty and there were just too many areas where there was little to no reception. All he could guess was that it just wasn't cost effective for the cell companies to run the necessary towers through the mountains to improve the signal strength. One thing that many did not know with cell phones, especially in the backcountry, was that they worked on a combination of signal and landline – Which meant that if one or the other were down for whatever reason you could have a failure to connect with your cell phone receiving that no signal icon on your phone.

With a few more incidents of sliding on the buried ice he finally pulled off in front of the small café. He had always laughed when he saw the name of it, "Take a Break Café". He remembered asking the owner how in the heck that name had been chosen. Faith had answered saying that originally the name had been simply Hillstown Café, but as customers who were passing through would comment, the one consistent comment she heard or got from them was, "This is a great place to take a break." So after hearing it so much she thought that it would be a great name for the café. It had also made it easier for people to remember it, and she and her staff had always tried to keep the food good and down home, and the atmosphere as friendly as possible. She and her husband had run the operation for something like 25 years, and their family were almost a landmark in themselves as they had been here for a couple of generations. Their cook Joseph who had been working there for at least 15 years had been someone that originally was passing through like so many others, but had broken down, and with very little cash at the time had in the end decided to stay. He had been a minor chef in some restaurant, and had asked Faith if she needed a cook. At the time Faith's husband Ron had been cooking, he being a short order cook from the past. They let him fix a couple of meals, and then hired him on the spot. Funny thing about Joseph lay with him only wanting to be called by his full first name. Said he hated the nickname Joe. So once the word got around no one ever did. The waitress on duty this day was Heather, she was just out of high school, and not sure what to do with her life yet, and was working there part time to assist her family in covering the bills that always seemed to arrive. Faith had made it a point to hire local high school graduates to work as either waitresses or bus boys. She was adamant about making sure where she could that the local younger generation had work. Faith was tough but fair.

About this time as these thoughts were running through his mind he pulled up in front of the café and as expected found no one parked there. Looking around at the other buildings here they appeared to be just as busy, meaning if anyone was around at all they had come on foot. As he pulled into the parking area in front of the café he had a small surprise. As the surface here was even more icy than where had had just come from and there for a moment did not know if he was going to create a grand opening for the café or actually stop. But thankfully the SUV did finally stop when it hit the concrete block put there to prevent such a thing from happening. Sitting there for a moment and catching his breath before he got out, he informed dispatch that he had arrived at the café and would pass on whatever he found out.

When he entered into the café he found everyone watching him, and Faith said, "You know there for a moment I didn't think you were going to stop. I know it has been mentioned a few times that a new front would be nice, but I don't think I am quite ready to do that as of yet." This brought a chuckle to the few who were here.

Faith was a woman in her mid to late 50's who looked more like she was someone in her middle 40's, just a little over 5' 2" in height and slight of figure. She was one of those women that other women hated. Not because she was difficult to get along with or had a personality quirk, but even though she had 4 children, who were all grown and on their own, her figure was one that always gave the appearance of never having carried. When asked about what she had done to make it that way she always would reply, "Nothing at all. I guess it is in my genes. Some women never get stretch marks, other do, and when carrying some women have their hip bones spread to accommodate their baby, and after it is born remain that way, and I am one that doesn't. I can't explain it any better than that." Most likely she would probably be showing some gray hair by now but like most women had her hair dyed to conceal the gray. Her husband was just as outgoing and friendly as she, and they had built the business over the years. He was on the other hand 6' tall and around 200 lbs. Making quite a couple with him towering over her, and she looking up to him. Yet when one saw them together it was obvious they were meant for each other. They just worked well together on all levels.

Looking around he saw that indeed Heather was the waitress on duty that day, and again as he sized up the people in the room he could see the lack of confidence that she had in herself. It would change as time went on, but as of right now she was untested in life. Without those challenges of life there was nothing for her to test herself against and find her own strengths and confidences. Yes she had the bravado of youth, but there was nothing behind it to support it. Other than Joseph, there were two customers there, both locals, and both operating the other retail establishments that this town had. Phil, who owned and operated the feed store combination hardware store, and Bob, who owned the gas station across the road were at the counter. "So", Faith asked, "TD would you like a cup of coffee?" TD stood for Terrance Davidson, and somehow Faith had just started calling him that and it had stuck. So to everyone in the community he was simply known as TD. "Yes that would be great, and your parking area is iced over, not that you didn't figure that out. I really wasn't sure it the vehicle was going to stop or not. And I was creeping in here, glad I didn't come in here with any speed or your concrete abutment might not have stopped me as I unexpectedly slid on that ice."

"Yeah, I think we all could see that. But until this second storm quits there isn't much we can do, and besides I don't see any other cars out there other than yours. Most are walking in, and while we've placed material down to try and keep the walkway from freezing even its still is a bit icy."

He went to the counter where Heather had then placed a cup of coffee for him. Taking a sip he said, "Ah that does hit the spot on a day like this. Okay, you are aware of why I am here, and Bob I don't know if Faith relayed, to you, our phone conversation, but I need to have you look at this photo also. This person should have come through here yesterday, if she made it this far. She is missing and I suspect that with this second storm so close on the heels of that last one that she probably hit some black ice somewhere and went off the road. But right now we are trying to determine how far she may have gotten before it happened." He then took the photo and passed it around. They all gathered around him at the counter and studied the photo, and Heather commented that she hadn't worked yesterday so she couldn't help but thought that this girl couldn't be much older than what she was. Looking at the picture Bob commented, and asked, "Is that her car that she is standing in front of?"

"Yes, that was what I was informed. Metallic Green 4 door sedan, just about 6 years old, but well cared for."

"Pretty little thing isn't she . . . it was really quiet yesterday, and that's unusual for a Saturday . . . yes I am almost sure she was in. Filled her car and bought a fountain soda . . . Seemed real excited to get back on the road. I think she drove across the road from here."

"Let me have a closer look at that." Faith said. "Yes she was here. Just about 5' 4" tall and I would guess around 130 lbs. Like most of us she dyes her hair. We talked a little since there wasn't many on the road, and I asked why she was with such a storm just ending, and roads barely cleared. She seemed excited. She said that she was on the way to see her fiancé . . . real impatient too. I think she said something like; it had been at least a month since they had been together. I think she had said something about a June wedding. She never reached her destination . . . too bad, I mean she was so looking forward to this, and then to have it end this way." Looking up from the photo she asked the obvious question. "Do you think she'll be found before spring?"

"Hard to say, but I think this second storm has given her less of a chance to survive, or for anyone to find her, if she's still alive. Now this is the tough question, since she was just passing through like so many others, do either of you remember how soon after she left that this second storm hit?"

Bob and Faith looked at each other and shrugged with Faith saying, "That's hard to say . . . maybe an hour, or maybe a little less." She was silent for a moment, "Couldn't have been much more than that."

"That sounds about right", Bob responded, "couldn't have been much more than an hour."

Thinking about the information he had received TD thought, *probably within fifty miles of here then. But that's still a lot of road to search, and until this storm quits no one will be doing any such a thing at all.*

"Oh yeah TD, I got a call just a short time ago from this girl's family." Faith replied, "While you didn't mention it, her name is Cathy, and they were trying to do the same thing you are. You know, narrow down the area that she might be in.

Considering the total distance she was traveling to shrink it down the area to probably within fifty or sixty miles is a help."

"Bob I know your part of the local search and rescue here, I'll keep you informed of what is going on, and kind of put the members of the team on the alert so when things break we can go out and search. In fact let's set up a meeting with the team tomorrow morning at the firehouse, the usual time would work. I think I'll head back and see if I can talk with the family on the phone. They may have some information that could help, and any help is welcome. And those updates are important." Paying for the coffee, he turned and thanked them all and told them he would keep every one informed of the progress. Yet he held out little hope of a happy resolution to the situation. The weather was just too bad and it was extremely cold. He felt, again that once she was found that she would have died from exposure due to the frigid temperatures. In truth he hoped that she had been killed by the crash. It would have been more humane for it to happen that way. But too often it was the other way around. They survive the crash only to succumb to the elements. He knew that the local search and rescue team would be preparing their snowmobiles, as it was the only way to safely get around in these conditions. Again he knew that until the storm broke and the conditions improved no one would be going anywhere.

On his way back to his residence he made a side trip to check on the young widow, and her children, and saw that their wood supply was getting thin. He knew that wood was the only way they heated their home. He would need to get the word out and have more delivered as soon as it was safe to do so. Overall Hillstown was a good town and took care of their own. So he knew that once word got out of this family's need that it would be taken care of, and taken care of with little fanfare and no one looking for praise. Of course he was heavily involved in making it happen. After all he was a family man and believed strongly in family. He got out of the SUV and checked in on them. When he saw the young widow she looked tired, but seemed to be doing okay. They passed the brief time with small talk and what was happening locally, and as he left he promised to continue to look in on her and her children as he could. As he pulled out and back on the road he thought that if she was just a bit younger she could have been his daughter. He and his wife Laura had been married for 18 years and their oldest child, a girl, was 16. They had a total of 3 children with the youngest a boy, at 10 years old. He believed that this young widow could be no more than 22 or 23. He did hope that she would find another to replace her loss, but that was something only time and God would bring to resolution. So in the present, the community kept her in their care.

Eventually he pulled back into his own residence and entered into their home and brought Laura up to date on what he had learned. He knew that he and his wife made a pretty good team, and that she had helped him with her insight on many of his cases over the years. "So Laura", he asked, "if you found yourself in this situation, as a woman, what would you do?"

"Well, I'm a bit different than the one who is missing."

"Different, how so? After all she is a woman out there all alone, as you would be, if it happened to you."

"True", Laura replied, "but I am older for one thing, and the big difference is that I grew up in the country and understand much of what would be necessary to survive. From what I have heard this one is strictly a city kid, and as such would know very little about surviving in the wilderness, and what kind of things she would need to do. So while I hold out hope, as you do, and I really do hope she's alive, I really feel, sadly, that if she's alive now, that with this storm being such a bear, she won't last the night. Besides, let's get real here for a moment, if she did have an accident there is really little chance she survived the crash anyway. I feel for the families involved here, and especially her fiancé, I mean I really feel for her fiancé, but the truth is I think it's probably a lost cause. I do hope that I am wrong. I am sure prayers are going out for her safe return, and if she is to live through this it will only be because of God's will."

"I guess this is all conjecture anyway. I have alerted Bob to have the search and rescue team ready once this storm breaks. After I talk to the family, I'll call dispatch and bring them up to date. Have you heard or seen anything on this storm while I was out?"

"From what they are saying the earliest this storm will break will be Tuesday, and that will be going into the fourth day of her missing. Even with what I know it would be difficult to make it that long without help."

"You're right, but until we know differently we still have to consider this a search and rescue and not just a recovery."

* * *

The rest of Sunday slipped quietly by with snow falling lightly every once in a while, with the skies still threatening. No additional word of Cathy ever reaching her destination, and as Sunday had progressed towards night the temperatures had continued to drop furthering the belief that in the end this would become a body recovery and not a rescue. As darkness approached the skies again were threatening heavy snow, and the winds were picking up adding to the cold. Would this missing young woman not only last out this night, but have the ability to survive an additional day and night before anyone could go search for her? That was the question on everyone's mind. They truly did not know if they had been in her situation if they could have survived.

The previous storm had been light and had shown promise of being the last of the season. After about nine months of overcast skies, rain and snow, they were ready for some real sunlight. So, after the weak storm had died out almost everyone was anticipating good weather. But, as usual, winter had a different idea. It was as if that cartoon from the 30's had become reality. As he sat there looking out on the surrounding countryside he thought about it. Turning towards Laura as he heard her approach, he could see the worry in her eyes, and again he could see that she was watching and waiting to see what this storm would do and when it would finish. "Looks quite nasty out there. At times I think it would be nice just to be able to hibernate like the bears do. Then you miss all this bad weather."

Smiling he said, "Yes, then we wouldn't even notice the cold. You know this storm kind of reminds me of that old cartoon 'To Spring' our kids used to love to watch when they were really young. I have to admit that it was one that I always enjoyed. I mean we all are here waiting for winter to end and when this storm hit with the strength it has, it brought back the struggle the elves had trying to tame winter. And of course winter putting up a terrible fight to stay."

"Yeah, very true, I can remember them laughing as the tug of war between winter and the elves would continue through most of the cartoon, until the elves were finally successful bringing spring to life. Yes I can see why this storm would bring that back to you. It does remind one of such a struggle. With this one and how strong it appears it's like winter saying I haven't released you yet. Yes spring is on the way but I am still in control right now."

Putting his arms around her waist, since he was behind her, and she resting her head on his shoulders and then looking out again as darkness enveloped the area he asked, "I wonder, is she still alive out there?"

Laura looking up at her husband over her shoulder replied, "I know you don't expect an answer as there is no way I have the answer. Only God really knows, and that at this point is between her and him."

Then turning her around and taking Laura in his arms and holding her he said, "I know you're right, and again it was a question that I knew you couldn't answer. But it has always been something that bothers me. In these situations if the person or persons are alive, you know that they are more or less helpless to do much and are expecting someone to come and rescue them. And that's part of my responsibility, so these things have always left me with feelings of failure when we finally find them. Many times you could see that they had survived, only to succumb just before they are found. Then when you see this you always end up second-guessing yourself. You know if only I was there quickly, or if they had been found a little quicker maybe there would be a chance that they would be alive now."

"Very true and this is one of the things that I love about you. You care and you always second-guess yourself . . . Always trying to find some way to make it better, or to come up with some quicker solution. It shows in your entire being. And it shows your faith in God and maybe not as strong, but your faith in your fellow man. I know in your job you see both sides of us – the bad, and the good. And I know, at times, I can tell that you can become depressed because you've seen too much of the bad. But I know that it only lasts for a short time and then you are back to who you are. I know that once this storm is over that you will be out there with the search and rescue team trying to do your best on finding this missing girl, and I would expect no less from you."

"Thank you for that. I know at times that I kind of become single-minded, one way, and just push ahead hoping to have a positive outcome to a bad situation. I know that at times because of this I have a tendency to shut you out as I concentrate on the problem, but understand that you are always there in the back of my mind. Always the one I will come back to, and will always value your word even if at that moment I don't show it." Again looking out into the night he could see that once again it was snowing. "I do hate the wait knowing that every second can mean the difference here. Yet, at the same time, knowing that by rushing into something like this we could end up with more than just one lost individual. So I wait."

"What else can you do? I worry for her also. A woman lost in this snow country and this storm and by her self, how horrible and scary, and she probably realizes that until this storm breaks that no one can come and try and find her. That's of course if she's still alive."

"Yes, there is that. She may have been killed immediately and so I could be worrying for nothing, but I have this nagging feeling that keeps telling me she is alive and struggling. And, that makes me all the more eager to get out there and find her. The conversation I had with her family informed me that she is a strong willed individual, a bit impatient, but I guess most of us are in our youth. I let them know that until the storm broke nothing much could be done. They said that they understood that, and knew that it was in God's hands. I had to agree with that. Right now it's beyond anything we can do. They said that they would continue to pray for her, and then added that they would be praying also for the rescue team when we go out searching. All I can say is that God will have to be involved if she is to survive, and she had better be strong otherwise there will be no chance."

"I noticed your cup is empty, would you like a refill before I shut it off and set the pot up for tomorrow?"

"Yes, that would be wonderful, and Laura, thanks. I think I needed to put into words my feelings and you seem always to know how to bring it out."

Smiling she said, "Your welcome, of course. Now, was it yes, for the second cup, or yes to set the pot up for tomorrow? Hey, we have been together long enough that I think we can read each other quite well and generally know when to do things, and I could really see how this one has grabbed you. Of course if you're interested we can get close tonight, as it is a cold night and I could use your closeness to keep me warm. That's of course, if you're not too distracted."

"A wonderful offer, and I'll probably take you up on that, but I've got some paperwork to finish before coming to bed, so if you are still awake when I get there we can enjoy each other's company. And it's yes on the second cup, thank you."

Smiling and shaking her head she said. "Okay then, one of the problems of being an adult is responsibility. I do hope to see you shortly." As she left and brought back his cup of coffee she gave him a suggestive smile and then headed for the bedroom.

He got up, sighed, shaking his head as he watched Laura leave. He reluctantly headed for the room that had been set up for an office, and sat down. He was behind on this stuff, actually he had admit that it was more than a little behind. It seemed that there were more hours involved in the paperwork than an arrest or ticket issued, or just reports on expenses and needs, and it turned out to be close to midnight when he finished his work. Tired he got up and headed for the bedroom and walked quietly in. When he had noticed the time he figured Laura would be sleeping, even though he knew that she would try to stay awake. And indeed she was asleep. So as quietly as he could he undressed and climbed into bed. The day ahead would be busy as he wanted to get the search and rescue people together and start working on their plan of attack so that once the storm broke they could be out there immediately. As he lay there he thought again: *Yes being an adult at times really did suck.*

Cathy – Sunday Night / Monday Morning

Looking back on Sunday, it had been a very cold and miserable day. It just seemed to have dragged on forever. She had tried to avoid having to make another trip to the copse of trees, but eventually had to give in to it. She thought that her second trip would have been easier, but instead had found it more difficult. Why was this so, she didn't know. Every time she had to use the cup she would hold it until the urine got cold and then would place it in the trunk where it would eventually freeze making it easy to remove from the plastic cup. She definitely was becoming very intimate with that hockey player's image that was on the cup. Well at least she still had a sense of humor. The real person probably would be shocked at what the cup was being used for. Yes hockey season was over, but she knew that in such small places where she had picked it up that their supplies of such things probably overlapped into many of the different sports seasons.

She now had everything she had brought with her on, and had looked for more. She also had finished taking the materials off the front seats, and was thinking that maybe with some work she could get the carpets up also, but thought that it might make it colder inside the car as they at least insulated the floors. As darkness had approached she had gotten out another candle and lit it for light. The flame only flickered slightly showing that even after the crash the car was somewhat airtight. The winds outside her car was picking up again and moving the trees and shaking her damaged makeshift shelter. Making her quite uncomfortable and still left her wondering if the car would remain wedged against the tree. With the windows now completely covered in ice she could not see out at all. But the winds were increasing rapidly in strength and were almost howling. She could hear the snow being blown around and suspected that once again that it was snowing. Temperatures appeared to be dropping again. This storm was strong. *Where had it come from anyway?* The last one appeared to be mild and really did seem to signal the end of winter. But now she knew how wrong she had been.

She had never been this cold in her life and it seemed that no matter how she tried she could not find any way to get any warmer, and had no idea on how to improve her condition. If she had worried that she was going to survive the night last night, she now worried even more. The storm seemed so much stronger and colder now. And while she had water and food, her spirits were down and with no one to talk to or with, things just ran around her mind. She had listened to music on her mp3 player until the batteries had died, and now had nothing to help her pass the time. One thing for sure she had come to a decision that if it quit snowing tomorrow she would leave and head back towards that town. *What was the name?* Thinking at first it did not come to her, but she did remember the restaurant she had stopped at. It was, "Take a Break Café", and it was located where? Well it didn't matter she knew that as strong as this storm had become that there would be little chance of anyone coming out to find or rescue her. And she was realistic enough to know that they wouldn't even know where to look anyway. When she had left on Saturday she had a 10-hour trip ahead of her, and she could have had this accident anywhere along her route. When she had realized this it added to her fear and her depression. This led her to once again pray a small prayer. She still wasn't sure if there was a creator, a God that would be that personal, but she had absolutely nothing to lose by trying. "God if you are real, please help. I am scared . . . really scared and I don't know which way to go, which way to turn. I don't know if this is where it is supposed to end for me, or if there will be more to my life." For a moment she broke down again, and then continued. "God I am completely lost, help me make the right decision here, and please, please be with my parents, and especially Keith. I know that they are very worried about me, and I can't even let them know that I am alive."

Again, she felt better about putting things into actual words. If there wasn't a God then at least she felt better about saying what she did. For a short time she almost felt peaceful as if somehow this God had heard her. Truthfully she had no proof one way or the other. So with no other feeling coming she hunkered down for the night knowing that there would be little sleep, and the night would probably seem like it would last forever. Holding her hands over the tiny flame she could feel the heat. Although it wasn't great it was warm. She then thought. *If I am careful I can hold this candle inside my emergency blanket and get what little heat it has to me.* She then took the candle and brought it to her, and like when she was a kid, put the blanket over her head and formed a small tent with it. While she was much larger now than when she was a kid, and the space under the blanket was tight it did work, and she could feel the heat coming off of the tiny flame. She had to be careful, as she couldn't allow herself to fall asleep while she did this, and she really did not know if this arrangement would make it dangerous with a buildup of carbon monoxide. At least with the candle she doubted it.

"Wait a minute here. Why didn't I think about this before?" She said softly. She had just realized that there was that single burner camp stove in her backpack. And while she knew that the fuel for it was small, if she was careful she could use it sparingly and maybe make it through the night by alternating the candle under the blanket and the cook stove in the car. And with a great supply of different ways to light them – the candle and stove – she at least did not have to worry about being able to do just that. Now excited she once again placed the candle on the rear shelf and then using the flashlight dug out the stove and propane bottle. It took her a little time and much shivering in the cold to finally get the propane bottle attached. She found that her hands were completely numb and had not sense of touch so something that would have normally been easy had become very difficult. Almost crying from wanting to get this thing lit, and feel the heat off of it she again fumbled with the knob that turned on the gas, and then used one of the cigarette lighters to ignite the gas. Only to have it die right back out. Thinking that she may have done something wrong she tried again and found that this time it stayed lit.

Immediately she dropped the lighter, and put her hands over the welcoming heat as it rose from the small stove. Now very carefully she drug it close to her and felt the welcoming heat slowly warm the inside of the car, the blanket, and her clothes. Now she knew that she would have to worry about carbon monoxide, she thought from her lessons that this gas was heavier so if she cracked open the door on the downhill side she should be safe. And at least if she was very careful and kept the stove turned down as low as she could make it go there would be a chance that she could use it most of the night. But if she did, then while she used it, she had to remain awake.

The night dragged as she found that as she warmed up that she would begin to doze. So as sleep would become overwhelming she would shut down the little cook stove and fall asleep until either the cold or the winds throwing something against her car or shaking it that she would then find herself wide awake once again. During those periods of sleep she had dreamed – my did she dream. In one she was a little girl again and was at a friend's house during the summer and enjoying the swimming pool as she and her girlfriends enjoyed a hot Saturday by the poolside. She did not know why her parents never wanted one, as they were so much fun and a great way to cool off in the summer. Another was while she was in high school and was so embarrassed by her parents. After all they were just so old fashioned and not what was happening now. How she had been almost unwilling to bring friends over since she didn't want any of her friends to see those dreaded plaques that were all over the house – so she had made excuses. Then ever so briefly she repeated the one from the first night of making her destination and almost seeing Keith. Then there came one from one of the family's summer vacation where they had traveled to some of the National Parks in the west. They had gone to Yellowstone, and then finished at the Grand Canyon. While both were neat to see, they had only held her interest for a short time. She really had wanted to be with her friends.

When she had awoken from this one she realized that in many ways she had tried to separate herself from her family and their faith in God for a long time. She now was becoming aware of the importance of family in one's life. In fact she found that if she allowed it that she and her mother probably would have a very special relationship that can only exist between a mother and daughter. "Mom, if I live through this I promise you to get closer to you. I have been such a fool trying to distance myself from you and dad, not realizing that you are so important to me." While being isolated as she presently was, she found that she had plenty of time to think and to put things in perspective. She was guessing that the dreams she were having was her mind trying to put things in proper order so that she could then view them and understand. She now knew that the only reason she was still alive was because of her dad's concern for her and making her put that emergency pack in her trunk. Without it she would have died that first night, and she knew it. Well if she did survive she had much to make up for. And that still was an unknown, as this storm had yet to break. And until the storm did break, there would be no one out looking for her, and from the sounds outside of her car there didn't seem to be a chance that it would break soon.

Once the morning arrived she felt that because of her diminishing supplies that she probably would run out of most of everything sometime that day. She saw that the kit had been put together for one to have supplies for about 3 days, and tomorrow would be that 3rd day. She had to get out even if she had to do it herself. And right now it looked like the best answer. All she would have to do is backtrack through those trees, then find a place that she could get back on the road, and walk back to that town. How far could it be anyway? She couldn't have been on the road more than thirty to forty-five minutes, so what would that be distance wise? Maybe if she pushed hard that there would be a chance that she could find one of those houses that were somewhere between here and that town. Of course this could only happen if it quit snowing and it looked like it might hold off. She knew she wasn't experienced enough to know how to fight her way through a snowstorm. Suddenly a large gust of wind really shook the car and the tree that the car was wedged against, for a few seconds she panicked as the car moved and briefly appeared to be sliding. "Oh no!" She cried. But the winds subsided for a short period of time and everything settled back down. She could feel her heart racing, and in the silence after the wind stopped she heard a groaning from her car. Then the winds picked up again and all she could hear were the winds, the snow and ice hitting the windows and body of the car. It was still dark, sometime during the night, and she found that once again that she was cold. She lit off the camp stove once more now worried that her limited supply of fuel had to be running out. She was using it as conservatively as she could, but how long could that one bottle of propane last? Again she had to admit that she had no idea. But the idea of running out with it as cold as it was really worried her. To have found a heat source then lose it probably would be worse than having never found one in the first place.

With the flashlight she dug in her pack and found a packet of hot chocolate, and then using the stove she heated some water mixed the cocoa in and then drank it. She could feel the warmth entering her body and had to admit is was nice to be able to put her cold hands around that warm tin cup. She was finding that a simple thing like this was almost a luxury right now.

Who would have thought it? This a luxury, you have to be kidding, right? But right now it really was. Once again comfortable, she found herself falling back to sleep. So once again she shut down the heat and fell asleep. Immediately she began dreaming again. She was a child again, and this time she and two of her friends were in the auditorium – lunchroom that she remembered from her time in elementary school. It was here the school assembled, and if they needed to watch something, they also assembled here. Only this time there was only the three of them, no adults, no teachers – nobody to bother them at all. Looking around she could see the curtains to the stage were open, and all the exit doors were closed. The tables that they used for lunch were all in the walls locked so that the floor was open and vacant. There was nothing around that could be hurt by them if they were deciding to do any mischief. And what kid wouldn't want to do such a thing when there was no one around to observe him or her, and place the responsibility of any damage directly to them.

Unknown at this time in the dream was a set of stairs to the far right. One of her friends was sitting and reading something and ignoring what she and her other friend were doing. In their hands they had ordinary coat hangers and were having fun throwing them around. Watching them slide across the floor, or alternately trying to hit the ceiling far above them. They were having such fun doing something they were not supposed to do, but at the same time they would not leave any damage behind showing that they had been breaking the rules. The one friend that had been joining her in this horseplay finally tired of it and left, leaving only herself and the other friend Carol whom continued to read. Carol suddenly jumped up and yelled, "I've become a student!" Carol then ran to those stairs that until this moment had been unseen, and rapidly ascended them. She yelled to Carol not really sure what she meant, "Student, what do you mean?" With no answer forthcoming she ran after her up the stairs. It seemed to go on forever and she found herself tiring rapidly, and stopped to rest. But her friend Carol never looked back or slowed down, but continued her rapid climb. Catching her breath she took off after her again and then looked back down and noticed that they were very high and where they had been previously was no longer visible. In the distance ahead and above her, she could see the top and knew that she would really be seconds behind her friend. She had somehow made up some of the distance between them. She saw Carol reach the top and could see a large smile on her face. In fact she almost seemed to glow with happiness. Then as she personally watched, four winged beasts picked up Carol just as she had reached the platform. These winged beasts carried Carol across an abyss that was so large and deep that there was absolutely no way to cross. The size and depth made the platform she was on seem very insubstantial and she sat down carefully, not wanting to fall, as she watched her friend disappear in the distance. Then she noticed a land across the abyss and found it to be one of the most beautiful she had ever seen. In her heart she wanted desperately to go there, but knew she could not as the only way across was to be carried by those winged beasts. She then heard herself say, "Only students and teachers can go there, and I've just missed." When she had made that statement she knew that she was neither, and almost cried, desperately longing to join her friend. At this point she awoke. The dream had seemed so real and where did it come from? While the school scene was something from her past, the rest was completely unknown. Then once again a couple of Bible verses entered her mind, "For all have sinned and fall short of the glory of God, and are justified freely by his grace through the redemption that came by Christ Jesus." Romans 3:23. Jesus answered, "I am the way and the truth, and the life. No one comes to the Father except through me." John 14:6.

She noticed that it was still night and once again she very was cold. Again she had no idea how soon the dawn would come or even what time it was or how long she had slept. But one thing she did know and she felt it to her very soul, that this last dream disturbed her deeply. She knew it had some significance but at the moment could not understand it at all. Students and teachers, what was that all about anyway? Again lighting the small stove she warmed up, turned it off, and again went back to sleep. If she dreamed again she didn't remember. Her thoughts being, that by dreaming so much she should be exhausted just from the exercise she had done in them. Eventually with the stops and starts of being awake, and what sleep she did get, she was able to see a difference in the night. At first not sure but as time continued slowly she could finally see that it had to be dawn and she had lived through another night. It had not been a comfortable one, but thanks to that stove she was alive. Again she thanked her dad for making her put that pack in her trunk. She remembered him saying, "Now honey, this thing doesn't take up much space, and if you never need it then so be it. But what if you really do and you don't have it? This small thing can mean the difference between you not coming back to us alive or having a happy reunion because it was there for you. Consider it an insurance policy, and if nothing else consider it a favor for me." How could she deny him when he had put it that way? After all she was very close to her father – something about fathers and daughters also . . . Especially, as she looked back on it, when she was growing up. He had always seemed so strong and confident and always seemed to be there for her. And once again, now that she was an adult, she had to admit that he had made sure that he was there for her even though he wasn't physically with her at this moment. How she wished she could talk to him right now. The yearning went deep, but it was only she, her wrecked car, and the storm.

Sometime close to dawn the winds had died and it was calm right now. With the iced over windows she could not see out properly to see if it had quit snowing. Reluctant to do so, since it would cause her to lose whatever heat she had in the car she finally just did it, she opened her door and looked out. She found that the snow now was at the bottom of the door but from her brief glance could tell that at this moment it was not snowing. With her decision made she knew that she would be trying to save herself and head back to that small mountain town. And the more daylight she gave herself the better chance she had of finding either that town or one of the farms or ranches that were outside of it. She really doubted that she had enough fuel left from her little stove to last out another night, and she figured that her food would be running out also. She also had no idea how long this storm was going to last, and from the strength that it had shown so far; it might just go another week. This was time she knew she didn't have.

Monday Morning – Hillstown

The alarm went off early, and he struggled to come to life. It was 5:30 in the morning and had only been in bed around 5 to 6 hours. Through the fog in his mind, as he had been very deep in sleep when the alarm had gone off, he could taste metal in his mouth which was quite dry. Turning over he smiled at Laura and said, "That was a short night."

Turning towards him she yawned and answered, "Yeah, it seems that most of them are. I really missed you last night."

"Sorry about that, I really didn't think it was going to take as long as it did. And I actually didn't get it all done. Ran out of gas at some point and just had to give it up."

"I could tell. I looked in on you once when it was getting really late and I was starting to fade, and you were concentrating so much that I don't think you even knew I was standing there."

"Really? You're right I didn't. Oh well, guess it's time to get this day going. I'll go push the button on the coffee, so you can get into the bathroom ahead of me, and then I guess with that it officially kicks this day off."

"Yeah, I know its part of being an adult. Truthfully I think I'd rather stay in bed here with you and do that adult thing."

Laughing he said, "Lady you are most tempting, but as you said we are responsible adults and the day has begun for us. And if I don't get moving here at this very moment I might just take you up on your offer." Sighing he stretched and climbed out of bed. Turning around he smiled as he watched Laura struggle out of bed and head for the bathroom. Shaking his head, he thought, *I love her so much, and I have no idea what I'd do if she wasn't here.* He headed out to the kitchen and started the coffee. They had about a half an hour before the kids had to be up and begin the daily process of getting ready for school. It, after all, was Monday. Maybe if he was quick he could join Laura in the shower just so they could have a little closeness before the day really got out of hand. You know wash each other's backs and hug, feeling that skin on skin touch that he always looked forward to. But again realized that she probably would have already been in and out in the time he took to come up with the idea, as she would only be rinsing off more to wake up than anything else. Probably later today or towards the night she would take a full bath or shower while there was no one around and she had the time. But for now, as usual, life would intrude and time she had alone, or together with him was a rare event.

As he expected as he was entering the bedroom her heard Laura yell, "Terry the bathroom's all yours. I've got to work towards getting breakfast on for the kids. When you get out you can then shake them out of bed. They seem to respond better to your authority than mine. When you come back into the kitchen I'll have a cup of coffee waiting for you."

Yelling back he asked, "Is that all? Just the coffee?"

"For now, after all you blew that chance last night. So now you will just have to wait." She laughed, and continued. "I must admit it would be nice to be able to sneak off like some teenagers, but . . ." Shaking her head, she had a smile and a far off look in her eyes, "I guess even when we can take a vacation at this stage in our lives it is the whole family and not just you and me. I know that family is number one for both of us, but every once in a while I think, wouldn't it be wonderful to have a short vacation, just the two of us."

"Yeah wouldn't it. Okay I'm heading for the bathroom now, and then I'll get the kids up. I'm sure that I'll embarrass our teenage daughter since daddy isn't supposed to go in her room without permission, but I'll pretend that I was ordered by the boss to do it."

"Truer words were never spoken, but she is the hardest to get up in the mornings and I think daddy's authority just might be what is needed. I don't want them to be late and she can drag the rest of us down as she comes to life. I'll do a quick check before you do and at the same time I'll find out if the schools are closed. I wouldn't want you to walk in on our daughter if she was already up and began dressing – not that you haven't seen here in her birthday suit. And I know, her up, like that's going to happen. With where we are, you know you would think so, but it is a rare thing when it snows like this, especially this late in the winter. Fortunately, the schools are next to the firehouse so it is kept pretty clear around there. On that subject I think you're going there to meet with the search and rescue team, so maybe you could just leave a little early and take our kids and drop them off."

Putting a sad look on his face he said, "The sheriff reduced to being a school bus driver? What would the neighbors say?" Then laughing he continued, "Sounds like a plan to me. You know one of the things I like about being in a small town, and it can be something not to like also, is that you always know what your kids are up to." With that he left for the bathroom and she to the kitchen to get the day officially of the ground. It was going to be a very busy day for all of them. She had to admit that he was right. There was very little their children could do without the word returning to them about where they were and what they were up to. She remembered that from her own youth. She had often wondered how her parents always seemed to know what she and her friends were doing, and not thinking that like them the parents had their own network. She smiled thinking to herself. *Now the shoe is on the other foot and it is my children who are the ones under scrutiny.*

As she put the breakfast together, bacon and eggs with toast and jam this morning, she could hear the complaints as Terry invaded the children's rooms, with loudest complaint coming from the oldest daughter. She laughed when she heard "Dad!" coming from her room, and then Terry saying to her that it was time to get moving and if she didn't he just might get a bucket of cold water to get wake her up. Shortly he stuck his head in the kitchen and said, "Mission accomplished, ma'am, and that bacon smells wonderful." Smiling back at him, she thanked him and he left to get into his uniform. Shortly the three children came straggling into the kitchen to get breakfast, and now truly the day and the chaos that always accompanied the children was in full swing. There was some complaining from the oldest daughter about having to ride to school with dad in the sheriff's vehicle, but the two younger boys were excited. They always loved it and would brag to their friends about it. Such is the difference between boys and girls, and of course age. Sarah the oldest was at the point in her journey to be heavily into friends and somewhat embarrassed about her parents. 16 was a time for much change in a girl's life. Still both of them kept the lines of communication open, the discipline where it should be, and to be helpful and be there when it was needed. It really was a hard balancing act, but so far they felt that they had been successful – well, as successful as any parent could be. She had accepted Christ back when she was about 13, and seemed to be very serious about it, and while she was a normal teenage girl she seemed to want to follow the scripture and not what was popular at school. That was not to say that she didn't want to be popular, as most girls at her age do. It was just that she knew where to draw the line, and Laura was always happy when Sarah would seek her out for advice. She knew that later in life, if they had built a good foundation with each other, they would always have that special bond.

Laura heard the horn honking, knowing that it was her signal that Terry was waiting out in the SUV for the children. So she hurried them along and out the door, stood there for a moment, and looked at the mess left behind, and listened to the quiet after the chaos of happy healthy children in the morning. Sighing, she started the cleanup process, and then she would have an hour before she would have to get ready for work herself. Terry, waiting in the vehicle, was a little chilly, as the heater hadn't kicked in yet. So to leave a warm house and get into a cold car was always a shock. He had honked the horn to let Laura know that he had the car running and it was time for the kids to head out to the cruiser. And sure enough he saw the backdoor open and they filed out, and joined him in the car with Sarah taking the front seat and Terrance Jr. the middle child, and Robert, the youngest, named after his father taking the back seat. He thought. *If there was just some way I could tap into all that energy that our sons seemed to have, just maybe I could accomplish anything I wanted.* He suspected that when he was young like that that his parents probably had wished for the same thing.

Again, looking at his daughter made him think of both the young widow, and the lost girl. It would be so easy to have either happen to his child later in her life. Well at least with Christ as a foundation in her life she would have more than family to fall back on. The trip to the school took about 30 minutes of careful driving. Since this was a small town all the grades shared this one school. Although there was a fence that divided the elementary age children from the Junior High and High School age children to prevent any major bullying from some of the older bigger children. Once the children were dropped off he let dispatch know that he was heading to the local fire department, and would probably be there most of not all of the morning, working with the local search and rescue on plans for searching for the missing person once the weather broke. With that accomplished he headed out of the school parking lot, carefully driving around the vehicles and snowmobiles, as children were dropped off for the day. He knew that shortly Laura would be heading out to her job – her business really. She was a licensed daycare specialist, and with a couple other mothers in the community ran a daycare center out of the community center. The community center was located next to a small public park, which had the standard play sets. And wasn't too far from the school making it convenient for the parents, who worked outside of town or within the community, to drop off their children who were too young for either pre-school or school.

While overall the community was a working community, meaning it had working ranches, farms and small businesses, there weren't enough to support everyone who lived here. So, many of the residents commuted to jobs in the distance. If you took a population count for a hundred square miles it might equal two thousand. The community was part of the unincorporated backcountry, and as such the government that it was under was the county. The county provided police protection, which of course was his job, road services, and whatever health and welfare was required. The volunteer fire department received part of its funding from both state and county funds, and the schools, while local, were part of the county district educational system. Part of their support, as a community, came from recreation, as both a national forest and a state reserve surrounded them. While they were somewhat isolated, during the months that the campgrounds, picnic areas and lakes were open the main 2-lane highway that went through the town was always busy. It was only during the winter and late fall months that the roads were rarely traveled, except on the weekends of course, since there were a few ski resorts, and because of this, the roads were cleared only after the major thoroughfares elsewhere had been cleared. Still, overall, because snow was something the area expected every winter there usually was enough equipment that the road would only be unplowed for 5 or 6 days at the most. Right now with this unusual storm it happened to be one of those times.

As he thought about these facts, after dropping off his children, he had wondered where and why such a powerful storm had hit them so late in the season. Like just about everyone else around he thought the mild one that had preceded this storm was the last one and spring would be showing its face soon. But literally just after the roads had been cleared, within hours it seemed, this one hit and hit was such a fury one would have thought that it was mid-winter instead of the end. Finally pulling in front of the firehouse he parked where there was a space for law enforcement and got out of the cruiser, (A SUV to be truthful). He noticed his reflection in the glass window besides the door that led inside to the office area. He thought for one in his mid-forties he looked pretty good. His 6' 2" frame showed to still be in somewhat decent physical shape, and his 200 lbs. of weight seemed to confirm it. Yes he had some of the love handles that always seemed to develop, and there was some gray starting to show both in his hair and his mustache. Again shaking his head he thought, *just where has the time gone?* Thinking of his wife, Laura, he remembered when he had first met her. It had been a blind date that a friend had set up and had, as he was sure she was, been a little reluctant to go through with it. But his friend, who had set it up, stated that the two of them were just right for each other. He remembered, right up to the time to go out with her that he was trying to come up with some reason or excuse to cancel out, but finally just decided to go. After all it could be a fun evening, or even if it wasn't then at least he would know.

They had met that night, with friends, at a local restaurant, and once he saw her he couldn't take his eyes off of her. She was just about 5' 8", looked to be around 130 lbs., with green eyes and light brown to blonde hair. He could see that she seemed as shocked and surprised by him as he was with her. For once, it appeared that their mutual friends were absolutely right. Literally from that first date they had been together constantly and it was only been 6 months later that he had proposed to her, and as they say the rest is history, and 18 years ago. He found, to his surprise that as time with her continued that his love and commitment to her had deepened, and then 2 years into the marriage their oldest had been born, and life took another turn for them as now they were no longer alone with each other. Again shaking his head he really did wonder where the time had gone. Their oldest was 16 and youngest 10, and it seemed that it was only yesterday and they were changing diapers on Sarah, and now she was in high school. In another couple of years she would be graduating and probably heading off to college – a young woman in her own right.

Why had his mind taken this turn this morning? He realized that it probably had to do with this missing woman. A young woman early in her life looking forward to marriage in June and eager to see her loved one. Yes it still could have been Sarah. Putting it this way made him realize how frantic the families had to be. He didn't know what he would do if it had been his daughter. Knowing, from his experience that because of the severe conditions this storm presented, that nothing could be done until it broke, and every minute, every hour that she was out there was time against her living through it. This storm had turned out to be very nasty and a strong one and he felt that this truly had to be the ending one for the winter. Anyway enough on that train of thought as he entered the building, it was time to start putting a plan together that they could use when this broke on Tuesday, *if* the forecasts were accurate.

He had at least 30 minutes before any of the leaders of the team would arrive. So he took advantage of this time and set up the space so that they could view the areas where they would most likely begin their search. He also got the coffee going and then in his mind starting looking at each member. Bob was the one he had put in charge of the team when he had decided that it was something that was needed for the area. Bob was in his late 30's and single at the moment. He had been married sometime in the past and from what had been said it had been a fiery three years. Three years of much anger and fighting. It was never known what had attracted the two together in the first place, but when it ended Bob swore he would never test those waters again. Fortunately for both of them the relationship was childless. She left and was never heard from again, while he continued his businesses here. He owned the gas station-combination small convenience store, and during the sportsman and hunting months would run a seasonal guide service. He would take fishermen to isolated lakes and hunters into distant areas to hunt. And he also knew most of the hiking trails and would lead some of the tenderfoots on hikes. He was of average height, had brown hair was fairly good looking and had a farmer's tan during the time he ran his seasonal business. Truly an outdoorsman he just preferred it when he could get away and into the wilderness. Because of his knowledge of the surrounding area, and his abilities, he was the natural selection for the leader.

Jacob was the second in charge – just past his middle twenties, married with 2 small children. He and his wife Caitlin operated a small dairy farm, dealing exclusively in Jersey cows for the richness of the milk they produced. At times, a cow could produce almost half cream in her milk. Because of this, their product was always in high demand, even though it was he and Caitlin that handled the operation. During the heavy demand periods they would hire some of the locals, and if he or she had to be gone, they had a couple of steady people who would come in and assist. Jacob was just short of 6' tall and built. He had a heavy frame but carried no fat. He was strong and had endurance, all from working the farm, and as a youth had hiked most of the countryside around Hillstown. While he probably did not know the area quite as well as Bob, it would be a toss up to find out who knew more. He was a natural leader and was a quiet soft-spoken individual. Thinking before saying anything, well liked in the community, and willing to help whenever and wherever it was needed. He was a deacon in the local Baptist Church and had a great singing voice so was also part of the small choir that sang each Sunday. The two of them Jacob and Caitlin formed a strong Christian family and it showed in every part of their lives.

Paul, the final alternate leader of the group was one when you first met him would figure that he was just too much into having fun to have much responsibility, but once one got to know him, one realized that much of it was a front. If the truth were told he was a pretty deep thinker, but hid it behind the bravado that he presented to the world. Single at this time and probably close to 30 he actually spent more time on his own in the woods than he did in civilization. He was an observer and very little got past him. His passion, which came from his youth, was tracking – an important part of any search and rescue team. In a debate he could hold his own against just about anybody who decided to take up the challenge. At times some of those debates had spontaneously taken off at the café, and it had been fun watching the sparing that would go on between the participants. He was one who had to commute to work. But at least the place where he worked allowed him the time off for search and rescue work. It was rare to work for such a place. But it had turned out that many years in the past the owner of this company had a child who became lost during a family outing and it was the local search and rescue that had come in and recovered his child safely. So he had a passion for any that worked as a volunteer in a search and rescue team. The rest of the team was just locals who knew the backcountry and could join when needed.

With one of the larger folding tables set up he spread a topo map of the area; a very detailed map that included all the trails, roads, properties, boundaries, and probable areas of danger. It was also color coded to show where other rescues had been made in the past. It included marks showing the exact locations where these people had been found. Plus it had either a number or a letter tied to that mark. This letter or number would take them to a notebook that would go into the details of the search, the rescue or recovery, and what the individual of group had been doing. It also included the location where the individuals were before they became lost. They had marked and colored it to see if there was a pattern to where people had a tendency to get lost, and to where they were found. The lay of the land could force lost people to move unconsciously in a particular direction, and if found and if the individuals had a tendency to follow these slight directional changes then, and here was the hope, there would be a pattern and a grouping where they would be recovered. And the map did show a few such areas. So as they planned these operations these particular areas would be some of the first to be checked out. The details between the maps and notebooks would assist them in any plan they put together. Part of what he was doing before the team arrived was to eliminate areas that hikers and hunters would most likely travel. They would not normally be found close to such areas like a driver of a car. Who, on the other hand, you wouldn't expect to find in such areas where the hunters are located and this would save time and effort. With everything prepared, he said a short prayer for the success of the search before the members arrived. Now it would be a short wait.

Then smelling the freshly brewed coffee he went into the small kitchen and grabbed a cup, and while doing that heard someone arrive. He had an office here as well as home, and had been thinking of completing some of the never ending paperwork before any arrived, but now had to wait as someone was obviously here. He heard someone yell out a hello, and recognized the voice as belonging to Bob. "Bob, I'm in the kitchen, getting some coffee. It just finished brewing, and I think we are going to be drinking a lot of the stuff this morning. I got the heat going just a short time ago so it's still not quite comfortable here yet, but will be shortly."

"Sounds great, I brought some donuts. Always found that coffee and donuts went great together." Bob replied "Sure do, aren't you here a little early? Yeah, I know you always are. I don't think the rest will be here for at least 30 minutes, but at least with you here we can kind of get a head start on this."

"That's alright if you want to, but I usually get here to help set up anyway, and if I know anything about law enforcement there is always a ton of paperwork to do. And while I know our main purpose here is to plan for our work tomorrow, I can take over the setup while you tackle some of your work. When the other two arrive we can go at it whole hog then."

"Thanks for the offer; I think most of it is already set up. But I'll take you up on it anyway. I was about to head into the office to do just that when I heard you arrive. I've set up a folding table out in the bay close to the corkboard so that we have plenty of space to work this. I suspect that you can bring in the chalkboard to give us something to write down our ideas also." Then looking around the area he shrugged. "Okay, I'll leave it in your capable hands." Turning to head for the office

Bob stopped him by placing his hands on his shoulder, looked seriously at him and asked, "What's your feeling on this one TD? I mean it just seems with how strong this one storm is that survival from someone who has experience would be tough. So a tenderfoot like this one . . ." At this point Bob sort of just trailed off letting his feelings show in his body language.

"Yeah, I know what you mean. But for some reason, and I cannot tell you why, I feel she is still alive and fighting. I know I've felt this way before and been wrong, but there just seems a strong sense that this one is a fighter and is out there alone and alive."

"I hope you're right. I know that the families are counting on us to give them an answer one way or the other. And we both know they are hoping for a miracle and she will be returned to them alive and well. Okay then, see you a little later, I'll finish the set up." Bob turned and headed out to the bay and TD to his office to work some of the many piles sitting there patiently awaiting his hands to finish them. Thinking about Bob again, he knew that he was one of those rare individuals who took responsibility very seriously, and never shirked anything put his way. He was willing to help wherever it was needed, and most of the time did not need to be asked, but seemed instinctively to know. While rich by no means, his two businesses left him comfortable. But other than knowing about his one failed marriage, he was very private about his immediate family. Oh well, this wasn't getting any of that paperwork done, so he sat down at his desk and started in.

* * *

Before he knew it he heard voices out in the bay area and knew that the others had arrived. He looked up at the wall clock and saw that an hour had passed since he had last talked with Bob. Where had the time gone? Getting up and shaking his head he headed out and saw Jacob and Paul both with their backs to him talking with Bob. Bob glanced over and said, "Ah the bear has come out of his den." The other two turned around, laughed at the comment, and greeted him, followed by asking how everything was going – the normal small talk before things settled down and they got serious about their up and coming task. Grabbing a donut and a fresh cup of coffee he settled in and said, "You know why we are here, and if things go right for us tomorrow we will be out trying to find this missing person. She disappeared Saturday while on a trip to see her fiancé. With the sudden arrival of this storm that we are now experiencing there is a good possibility that she crashed because of it. This will be the third day that she had been missing, which means that she has spent 2 nights in this freezing weather."

"Does she have any cold weather survival training or experience?" Jacob asked.

"None that I know of. In fact, from what I have been able to gather, she is strictly a city kid . . . Hates the country, camping, and anything to do with the outdoors."

"So I guess", Paul added, "you are thinking then that this will be a recovery operation and not a rescue."

"Surprisingly, not so. I have a feeling that this woman is still alive out there. And I know I've had that feeling before and it has been proven wrong. I talked with her dad on the phone a little while ago and he stated that he had made her carry an emergency pack in her car for just such emergencies. So if she survived the TC, then she has some supplies to help her survive the weather."

"That's great, but with no experience, even with something to increase the odds of her living, it really has been cold the last two nights – midwinter cold." Bob stated. "I think that it would take much of what I know to have survived in these conditions that this storm has been dumping on us."

"She comes from a Christian family and there has been much prayer that has gone out for her safe return, and I put much credence in prayer." TD continued. "I have seen it work time and time again, and before you say anything Bob, I know that you have no faith in such things. Although with what you love to do and spend time in I will never understand that. How can you not see God's majesty while you are out in the woods? It's there everywhere that you are."

"Yeah, I've heard the argument a thousand times, but there hasn't been anything to convince me. I see the struggle between prey and predator, the struggle one has to survive, to know while it can be relaxing and recharging to go into the forest, it still is a dangerous world where you could become breakfast for some animal. Or by not being careful get lost and die because of exposure, or injure yourself in such a way that without assistance your injuries will finish you off. Anyway enough on this, we seem to go over the same ground every time we begin our planning. Shall we start? I know that this time, while there is much area to cover, we at least have a starting point. In other search and rescue operations we have had to guess."

"True, we can, at least I think we can, eliminate many of the areas as a place where she is not likely to be, and concentrate on others. I know that when we go out tomorrow that we will only have about a half dozen snowmobiles and searchers so we will have to be very sure of where we look and not try and duplicate another's effort."

"Obviously, since she was driving we can eliminate most of the isolated areas and concentrate strictly on any close to the road. Have you come up with an estimate as to how far she may have gone?" Paul asked.

"From the little information I could gather, and what I am to say here is just an educated guess, somewhere between 25 to 50 miles from us. And yes I know that's still a lot of ground to cover. But as you said it still eliminates many of the areas. What I want us to do right now is to look at the road, both on the map, and from our experience, and try to figure out where the danger areas are. You know areas where there's a chance for black ice, or unexpected slippery conditions, things like that. Once we figure them out they will be the areas we will concentrate most heavily on, but making sure that between those areas that we are still alert. You know, just in case something like an animal darting across the road caused her to leave the road. Not that there would be many out in this storm, but it does happen."

The four of them were silent for a while as they each thought about the road and how the conditions could change from moment to moment. It was suspected that some of the snow had melted between storms so there could have been a lot of standing water on the road. And with no one traveling there would be no tires to push the water off or heat the pavement to help evaporate the water. So as the second storm had approached there would have been plenty of opportunity for ice to form. As it approached, temperatures had dropped rapidly, and to someone driving it would not have been obvious until the vehicle they were driving started to slide. Once the traction had been lost it would have been too late to stop one from hitting something. There were too many curves, trees, and obstructions. When they thought about it, it was obvious that there could easily be too many spots on the road to narrow the search area down by much.

"Thinking about this last storm here", Paul commented, "and how it showed up on the heels of the last mild one, I don't know, there just seems like there is very little of this road that wouldn't have been a problem."

"Yeah I was coming to the same conclusion." Bob said. "We hadn't dried out from the last one and while we had some sunlight, which appeared to be doing a great job of melting the snow on the road, it left the roadway itself soaked. Then wham! We were socked with this one. It would have made the road an ice rink."

"Very true", Jacob added, "and the only warning that this was happening might have been some ice starting to form on the windshield. But that could have easily been dismissed as either slush being splashed on the windshield or ice dropping off the trees as it softened and lost its grip."

"So I guess we'll have to look at this from the distance aspect instead. As you all have just pointed out there would be no way to use known areas with as much water, snow and ice that would have been on that road. Oh well, I was hoping. So while I figured that she may have gotten at least 25 miles from here before trouble, I think now because of what the three of you have brought up that we will have to start much closer in." TD replied, thought a moment and continued. "Hmmm, do you think ten miles out as a starting point is too soon?"

The others looked at each other and then shrugged, with Bob then asking, "Who knows? It will definitely increase the time and distance we have to cover. But I would really feel stupid if the TC was that close and we started looking further out, and then later found that we had missed her because of something like that. What do you two think?"

Jacob shaking his head said, "I really don't know. With just six of us out there . . . hmmm, maybe it's a good idea, although I would suspect she's further out. But like you Bob, I would really be bothered if it were so."

"Okay guys here are a thought. I know that we normally break up and search separate areas so as to cover as much ground as we can. But because there is a slight possibility, and I mean slight that she could be in that close or even closer, let's have the whole team start here just outside of town, spread out and do a thorough search say out to 15 miles. It should speed the search in that area up considerably. Then once we are satisfied we can break down into the teams of two and work the areas we end up assigning each other today. And as we head out for that starting point we all can kind of watch for any signs of the TC happening earlier." Paul asked, "How's that sound?"

With the others nodding in agreement TD said, "Great idea, a really great idea. That would eliminate an area quickly, probably within a few hours or so. Then we could break the team up as you suggested, and work the areas where we really feel she might be. Either you, Bob, or Jacob have any better suggestions?" Again both shook their heads in the negative. They continued to work on the plans until TD looked up at the clock and said, "Okay then, we have a rough plan worked out here. I see that it's approaching lunch, so let's break for now. I'll see you all back here at around 1300, and we'll get into the final details and break up the areas." The others nodded in agreement and with that they took a break and headed out the firehouse door. With the community center close by TD decided that he would drop in on Laura for a couple of minutes and see if she needed anything before heading up to the café where he would join the rest of the team for lunch.

Cathy – Monday Morning

She awoke suddenly and realized that she had fallen back to sleep. After another cold and somewhat sleepless night she could see that it was now just past dawn. She had been dreaming again, and this time she had been reliving something from her past. If she remembered right she was around 10 when it happened. She and her mother had gone to the mall for some shopping, something she loved to do. Excited she ran ahead of her mother and opened the glass doors leading inside the enclosed mall and heard music. Stopping in shock, as this wasn't the music the mall normally played over their speakers, but a live group of musicians performing right there. It was a country-western band consisting of 4 members, and the singer was a woman with a strong voice. While this type of music wasn't her favorite she couldn't help but listen. Shortly her mother was standing next to her listening also. Other than the choir at church this was the only live group she had ever heard. When the song had finished, the singer stated it was because of God that she and the band were where they were today. She wondered how God could do such things. After all, this band sounded good, and it must have been their own work that got them here. Shortly after a couple of additional songs her mother gently pulled her away and they went to do whatever shopping they were here to do. She remembered that she could hear the country band in much of the mall that day.

As she thought about the dream and the incident from her past she had to admit that there seemed to be people everywhere that acknowledged this God. Why did she have such a problem with it? As she became more awake the dream began to fade away. Once again she filled the cup, and then carefully opened the door to look out and see what had happened over night. From her view she could see that there was some additional snow and the wind had blown much of it around into drifts. Right now it was calm and it wasn't snowing. While it was still overcast, with very little definition to the gray, there appeared to be a chance that any additional snow might hold off. "Well, Cath it's going to have to be today and very soon if I'm going to start my hike back." She had planned on it, but didn't know if she would do it. Yet at the moment everything seemed to say if she was, it would have to be now. Before dark the night before she had composed a couple of notes, one said, "I'm alive and it's Monday. I am leaving my car and heading back to find help . . . Plan on finding a way back to the road and following it back." The second was a short letter she had put together for her family if she didn't make it, and it said. "Mom and dad, I am sorry. I am trying to live through this but if I don't then this will have to do. Dad you told me that one day my impatience would get me in trouble and as usual you were right. Had I waited, then this probably wouldn't have happened to me. Mom, thank you for everything . . . I love you both and truly wish I could be with you at this very moment. Instead I am here lost in this snowstorm with no real way out. Bro' we've been the best of enemies and the worst of friends over the years. I love you Keith, I so desperately wanted to see you, and even after this accident dreamed of arriving there at your house and seeing you. We were to be married soon, and I so looked forward to us. I love you all, Cath."

This second note addressed to her family she had placed in an unsealed envelope that had been in the car and simply wrote "mom and dad" on the outside. She then placed the two notes on the dash and placed something heavy on them so that they would stay and hoped they would be found when her car was located. By the time she had finished writing them and then placing them on the dash it had become almost too dark to see, and she knew she had that cold Sunday night ahead of her . . . and, yes it had been a cold night, a very cold night, but she once again had lived through it, somehow. Now could she make the necessary hike to safety and put an end to this dangerous situation? She really did not know, as this was something she had no experience in at all.

* * *

Looking at the wreck that was once her pride and joy she started her hike away from the car. Again looking at the skies she could see that at least for the moment it seemed a little brighter even though the cloud cover was still formless and gray. At least it wasn't snowing and the winds seemed to be soft. Maybe it was a good sign that something might be breaking her way. Then unbidden to her mind another Bible verse flashed: "No matter how deep the stain of your sins, I can take it out and make you as clean as the freshly fallen snow." Is 1:18. Where had that come from? Maybe being in all this freshly fallen snow somehow had triggered it. She really had no idea that she had somehow memorized all this scripture. After all, it was something that wasn't important to her – or was it? Well enough for now, she had better be concentrating on what she was about to do. As she started the hike she found that as she cleared the car, the snow was just above her knees and was not easy to walk through.

In a short time, and in a short hike, she found that maybe this wouldn't be as simple as she thought. With the snow cover she couldn't really see what the ground was like underneath, and she was finding that the surface was uneven. Gritting her teeth since having made the decision, she just started pushing through. After all, how hard could it be to get around these trees, follow the edge of the road, and then find a way back up to the road where it would be much easier to hike? As she worked her way around the copse of trees that had been her bathroom she found that the trees had gotten heavier and closer together forcing her deeper into the woods and further from the road. Looking back she could see her tracks in the snow where she had broken a trail. She found that now with the exertion she was breathing hard and starting to warm up considerably. "At least I won't be cold." She told herself. Also seeing that she had left a plain and visible trail gave her confidence in that if her car was found then they would be able to follow her. Listening, it seemed that the forest was silent, as if waiting for something. The only sound she was hearing was her breathing – it was eerie and even somewhat spooky to have things this quiet. She actually started humming to herself to help relax her nerves. But after a short period of time she found that just the work of breaking a trail in the snow took all of her concentration and energy. She had fallen a couple of times already from tripping over something hidden under the snow. With these lessons firmly in her mind she was trying to be even more careful, but what could she do? There wasn't even a hint of what was under there. And for the first time Cathy felt the frightening possibility that this might take much longer than she expected. "Come on Cath', you can do this. Just put one foot in front of the other and go. You won't get there standing here and worrying about it."

After what she guessed was about an hour she found an area where a tree had fallen sometime in the past, and the area seemed somewhat protected. She needed a break, and had found that now she was sweating. So far she had been unable to work her way back to the road but was still confident that it had to be just a little ways off to her left. Again looking back she could she the trail she had broken disappearing into the distance. She looked down and saw that her pants were wet from the melting snow that had stuck to her, but at least for the moment her legs did not seem to be cold, and so far, her feet appeared to be dry. What would happen if her shoes soaked through? It would be uncomfortable and make hiking harder, but would it also mean that her feet could start freezing? That scared her, as it was something she hadn't even thought about or considered. She was now realizing that her decision to leave might not have been such a good idea after all. But after getting this far, she still wanted to get back to the road, which was her original goal. Besides she felt that now she had come too far to backtrack and admit defeat. It was better just to go forward and find help then to return to the wreck and hope that someone would find her.

Once she rested she headed out once more attempting to go left towards the road. But between the heavy growth of trees, and the bushes that were heavy in the area and covered in wicked thorns, she was forced to continue in a direction she was guessing that paralleled the road. Ahead and in the distance there appeared to be an increase in the amount of trees and found as she approached the area that she was being forced right and in her mind away from the road. Now what? It seemed that everything, even the trees were conspiring against her from making her goal. There had to be a way to get around this. There just had to be. She was guessing that by now it had to be mid-morning, and if that was true she really hadn't got as far as she felt she should have. Plus by now she had expected to be back on the road and having an easier time of it. But she wasn't, and it had been much harder work just to get where she presently was, wherever was, is? She found that she was tiring quicker, and that physically she was not in very good shape. That didn't make sense to her as she went to the gym and worked out all the time. She prided herself in being in shape and looking as good as she could. With that thought she laughed. *I probably look like hell right now. And look at this stylish outfit I am wearing – seating material from 6 years ago plus all these layers.* She laughed at her little joke. Well at least it seemed to have lifted her spirits a little. *Guess I better get going; sitting here will not get me out of here.*

Before starting again she looked ahead at that line of trees that kept pushing her to the right, shaking her head she thought. *I wonder if I force my way through this mess if I can find another pathway that goes to the left and the direction I really want to go. Hmmm, maybe I'll just go a little further this way and see if there are any changes. If not . . . then try at that point. What I really need to do is conserve my energy. I'm sure I still have a long hike ahead of me.* Steeling up the nerve and strength she headed out from her resting-place. She was getting a little chilled anyway, and she felt that it was much better being warm. She found that it was a still and silent white world, again as if it was waiting for something to happen.

The area she was presently in consisted of heavy growths of pine, cedar, and a number of deciduous trees. Without their leaves she could not recognize them at all, not that she was such an expert. *Again I leave landscaping to the ones who care. As long as it looks nice and seems to flow and is pleasing to the eye, what else is necessary?* Although the area she was presently in appeared to be untouched by man. An idle thought came to her. *I wonder if this is what the ones who put together those landscapes are trying to imitate what I'm seeing here.* There were many downed trees and some were quite rotten showing that they had been on the ground for a long time. She had noticed that presently she had been heading in a slight uphill direction. There were some hills that she could see off to her right but because of the height of the trees to her left she couldn't see what the land was doing at all. Now for the first time she understood the phrase, "You can't see the forest for the trees." The trees blocked her view of anything but what was immediately around her. The snow also continued to be a problem as it hid everything that lay beneath it. She had tripped, stumbled and fallen too many times to count. She had no idea if where she was hiking was actually a trail or path or she was just finding an opening and going where it led. *How did those mountain men do it back it their time? This is so hard.* She found that her flagging strength was leaving her rapidly, and there was no relief or signs that anything would be changing anytime soon.

Thankfully, up to this point, any additional snowfall had held off. But could she count on that continuing? Turning around again, she could see where she had been by the broken path in the new snow. She was surprised when she looked closely to see that she had not kept to a straight line at all. And she could see where she had fallen at least 3 or 4 times. What direction was she going in anyway? Again she had no answer to give herself. As far as she knew the road had to be just a short distance to her left. But these darn trees just refused to let her get anywhere close or let her break through. Heck it wasn't only the trees; it was those thorny bushes which she assumed was probably berry bushes of some kind. They were everywhere and in some places she could see that they covered just about every inch of the ground between the trees for just about as far as she could see. She seemed to remember somewhere in the depths of her mind that on a family outing that daddy had mentioned something about the moss on trees. But exactly what it was she couldn't remember. It must not have been much more than a comment anyway. She saw that these trees were just covered in it. That probably meant that this area got a lot of rain, snow and such. Well for one thing for sure, she could confirm the snow part. She had only been in the area for a few days and it was close to the end of winter and there had fallen too much of the white stuff as far as she was concerned. She found that her lungs burned, both from the cold and the effort she had to put forth just to work her way through the snow. It was tough, *so very tough.* Yet she knew that if she gave up, she would die. What a horrible thought, she could actually become no more and no one the wiser to where she was, *no one.* These thoughts brought up the emotions once again, and anger at herself for doing something so stupid. Still the anger gave her additional resolve that she wasn't going to die out here. She headed out again and began pushing through the snow and promptly fell in a hidden hole that came close to twisting her ankle. Catching her breath for a moment she got her anger and fear under control and said, "Now that was stupid Cath'. You let your anger get control of yourself there and almost finished it." Shaking her head, all she could do was pick herself up and start heading out once again, but being as careful as she could. *But how does one avoid unseen hazards?*

The winds began to pick up again and now she found that she was hiking into those winds. The winds were chilling her face and ears, and she had to reach up now and then to try and warm them with her hands. The hiking she was doing was very difficult, she found that she was breathing hard almost all the time, and her times between hiking and stopping to catch her breath were becoming less and less. She saw ahead of her that it appeared that the line of trees to her left was going to be forcing her further right, but there was nothing she could do about it. Then, in the distance, as she reached that shift pushing her further right, she saw an animal darting away from her. It appeared to be panicked as if it was running from something. And shortly after that something did appear. Catching her breath and sliding behind one of the many trees she watched as a pack of wild dogs, wolves, or coyotes dashed after the animal. She could see that they were running, what appeared to be a deer, or something like a deer, down. Not wanting to watch but at the same time unable to keep her eyes off the scene she watched them until they were out of sight. *Wow, and I thought the only danger I had to face out here was the cold and snow. That could have been me.* When she had thought that she realized that indeed it could have been her that the pack was chasing down instead of that deer. She could have ended up being a meal for them. She shuddered with this concluding thought. *Now, I've got to think even more and watch out. What else can be moving out here anyway? What else can be a danger to me?* She, waited a little longer, and then as quietly and as quickly as she could, crossed what she assumed was a meadow. It left her vulnerable, but most of the openness was to her right side in the direction those wild animals went. Carefully she hugged the trees to her left. Stopping half way across, she could hear the barking and yipping from the pack in the distance. Just ahead of her she could see where they had bounded out into the meadow and went chasing their prey. Would they catch the poor thing or would it get away? While she kind of hoped that it would escape, she knew that if it did that the pack would still be hungry and on the hunt. And if they came back this way they could pick up her scent and then start hunting her. If she wasn't scared before, this thought really scared her. There was no way that she could outdistance them, just no way.

The winds continued to pick up in intensity and shortly it was howling again, and there was a feel in the air that said it was about to start snowing again. Now what could she do? She no longer had the protection of the car and was out in the open. She was going to have to force her way into those thick stands of trees and get out of the wind. It was sucking what little heat she had right out of her. But there was a dilemma, as she also needed to get out of the area of the pack. Both were necessary if she was to survive, and she wanted so desperately to live. With the pack out of sight, and with the winds now blowing as hard as they were, she could no longer hear the pack. So at this point thinking that she was in more danger from the cold winds she dropped her cautiousness and picked up her pace to find a place where she could get out of the winds and the returning snow. How far had she come since she had left her car, and what time was it? She really had no idea, none. She hoped that she had covered most of the distance she had to go, but again had no idea. She had to admit it now, with what the heavy stands of trees and those thorny bushes had done was to force away from her goal, and she was lost and knew it. Maybe she should have stayed with her car. But there was nothing she could do about that now. It was too far back and if it snowed, yes if it started snowing again, then it would cover her trail that she had broken. That's if the winds didn't do it first. She had no choice; she had to continue on and try to find some kind of shelter ahead of her in the unknown countryside.

In a short time she crossed the point where she had seen the chase come out of the woods. If there was a path or trail there she couldn't see one. Even if there was, there was *no* way that she would go down it, as that was where the pack had come out of the trees. So with some trepidation she crossed their exit point and continued ahead. Suddenly she realized that the tree line was changing direction and was even thicker still. She almost panicked again when she realized that now she was being forced into the direction that the pack had gone placing her closer to this danger.

Stopping for a moment and trying to get herself under control, she found that she was shaking. Shaking both from the fear that was rising unbidden in her and the cold. She found that she could not just stand here, and found that she was crying, and that fear continued to rise in her. Scared, really scared now she fought hard to get the fear under control. There was nothing she could do about the crying at this time, it was beyond her. It was as if she finally just let it go. She could feel the tears starting out warm running down her face and before wiping them off to be cold. She almost found herself frozen to that spot unable to move or think. When she looked desperately into those trees she found a large hillside there and large boulders that the trees were up against – leaving no doubt in her mind that there was no way to go through the trees here. She had no choice she had to go in the direction of that pack.

Because of her change in direction the winds that had been hitting her in the face were now hitting her on her left side. What could she do? The last thing she wanted to do was get closer to those animals. The winds were also posing a problem, as they would gust, it would knock her off balance. With the uncertain footing and the shifting winds, travel was becoming much more difficult, and she was already tired from the effort she had expended just getting to where she was, wherever that might be. She stayed as close to the trees as she could and worked her way in this new direction hoping soon that it would change and she could at least move away from those animals instead of towards them. In the distance between the blowing snow and the open snow covered meadow she thought she could just make out the pack. If this was indeed them, they appeared to be staying in one place for the moment. Then the fear that she had finally gotten under control threatened to overwhelm her again. She found that again she was being forced even closer to the pack as the trees and brush forced her even further to the right. "Oh God no, please no. Please . . . please help." She whispered. Yet the only sounds she heard were the winds blowing through the trees and the strong gusts as they hit her. Shaking from fear she carefully continued her hike and then suddenly came to the end of the trees in this area. Not truly the end but it seemed that the trees were slowly encroaching into the meadow and this was a finger of that invasion.

Hugging the trees as close as she dared she went around that finger and was immediately hit with the full force of the wind. It literally knocked her over. It was a surprise. She had thought that the force of the wind she had been feeling was as strong as it was going to get. Not realizing that the trees had been taking some of the force out of it. Now by working around that finger she found herself in a portion of the meadow where there were no trees to block the winds at all and as such left her at the full mercy and fury of the winds. She felt exhausted, overwhelmed, but fear drove her on. She now knew that if she didn't find a place to shelter there was no way she would survive, and she knew, now that for the first time in her life, she could really die out here. And it was her decisions that she would make now that could mean the difference. Again when the full reality of this hit her she said a small prayer, "I don't understand God, I just don't understand, why is this happening? Am I going to live? Help, just please help me live." She found herself shaking uncontrollably, and the tears couldn't be turned off. She knew that she was just about finished, and if she didn't find some place to go, some place out of these winds, some place completely sheltered that soon it would be done. She knew that she had to get out of this meadow. Here the winds were just too strong and cold. Then she realized, even in its fury, there seemed to be one small benefit. This part of the meadow, while it still had snow on the ground, was not very deep. It seemed that the winds had blown it away leaving only a small amount making the way less treacherous than where she had been hiking.

Ahead of her in the distance through the blowing snow she could see that the meadow was narrowing and forming a "V". As she struggled towards that point she found that sometime in the great past something had killed and knocked over a huge number of trees. They were piled haphazardly in every which direction and on top of each other. Around the edges of these dead trees young trees were starting to slowly replace their fallen comrades. At this moment she no longer was worrying about the pack, but only trying to find a way out of this dangerously cold wind. As she got closer to the "V" she found that the winds were even blowing harder here. She could barely stand. Maybe it was the winds that had blown these trees over sometime in the great past. When she reached this pile of dead trees the first thing she noticed was a lessening of the winds. They appeared to be blocking, at least partially, the force of the wind here. Looking closely she could see a number of places where she might be able to crawl under this mess and maybe be truly out of the winds. One thing for sure, as tired as she was, she could barely think straight. And right now there had been nothing behind her that offered any shelter and she did not know what was ahead of her. So this would have to do. Picking a likely spot she started to crawl into the pile. As she did the wind was blocked completely. Immediately she felt warmer. But there was no way that she could stay where she was at the moment. So she continued to crawl and through hitting a number of dead ends, and changes of direction, until she found herself somewhere towards the middle, or at least she thought it was the middle, an area that she could almost stand up in. There wasn't even any snow there and it appeared to be dry – a little oasis in the middle of a snowy desert.

Sitting down and leaning back against one of the logs she could feel the weariness in her very being and with the relief of being out of the snow and wind began crying all over again. She never realized that she had stopped crying. Emotionally she felt quite drained, and at the moment did not even have enough energy to even move. Staring out at nothing there was a ringing in her ears, and suddenly she awoke and realized that she had fallen asleep. She knew that she had been lucky that she had actually awakened. That could have been the end of it right there. And she would have never even known.

Hillstown Search and Rescue – Monday Afternoon

When TD finally dropped by the café to meet for lunch with the rest of the team the winds had picked back up and were promising to be much stronger. The winds were also getting colder adding the promise of more snow. With this final fury from the storm he was beginning to doubt, even with his feelings that this woman was going to survive this. This particular storm was just wicked and seemed bent on showing everyone that winter was still in charge here. As he entered the café the winds grabbed the door out of his hand and slammed it shut causing all inside to jump a little. Shrugging, he said, "Sorry about that . . .

Wasn't expecting the wind to grab the door like that. It just jerked it right out of my hand and before I could stop it from slamming the door."

Smiling at him from her position near the door Faith said, "Yeah we could see that. At least you didn't let out too much of the heat." Then pointing over towards the far end of the cafe she said. "The rest of your team is over there in the corner. They haven't said much so far, at least to rest of us. Your usual?"

"That would be great. We really don't know any more than when I was in here a short time ago. We are hoping for the storm to break tonight so we can get out there early tomorrow. While we are on that subject, can you come in here early tomorrow and feed the team before we go out? It would bring us all together and iron out any last second changes we would want to make."

"What time would you like this to happen?" Faith asked.

"I'd like the team out searching as soon as it is safe to do so . . . so how about 5:00am? And I want it to be easy for you so make it pancakes, hash browns, bacon and eggs, with plenty of coffee. And can you put some sack lunches together also? The total amount of members on the team this time will be six."

"You don't want much do you?" Then smiling Faith stated, "Of course, no problem, I suspect that I'll bill the normal channel here. So you are trying to be on the road by 6:00am if I have it right?"

"Exactly, and I'll have the team at your door here by that 5:00am so that we can get right to it."

"Okay then, it will be just Ron and me, as Joseph isn't due to come in until about the time you are leaving."

"Thanks Faith, it's important that we get off with a good start and this will help tremendously." He turned and headed over to the table where the other 3 members of the team were sitting and joined them. Bob stating, "I think we are in for one hell of a night. It looks as if we're heading into a blizzard here. You know one of those we get now and then in the middle of winter. It must be blowing somewhere around forty miles per hour out there right now and the gusts are pushing much higher than that. Truthfully I can't see our victim surviving this. And yes I know others have, so there's a chance she will. But I'm sure you felt how that wind just cut right through you and even made it hard to breathe. If it starts snowing again it will only get worse. I really do hope this thing blows itself out tonight some time. I for one am quite tired of winter, and especially this storm. I'm ready for a warm spring, and it cannot come soon enough."

TD could see that the others were in agreement, and he had to admit that he was truly ready for spring himself. With the previous storm being so weak all had felt that winter had finally blown itself out and spring was on the way. Then this one arrived and dashed all such hopes. He could see that the others at the table were waiting for their food, so he sat down in the one empty chair and joined them. Just where had this storm come from anyway? It had not been on anyone's radar or in any weather forecast. Yet it was here and strong. As they were waiting for their food to arrive TD asked, "I know that you three are going out in this search effort, but who are the other two that will be joining us?"

Bob answering said, "As you would expect, a couple of the locals who like us are quite familiar with the area. Give me a second and I'll give you their names. They have been with us before. Oh by the way, who will be your partner on this one?"

"I think I'll have Jacob join me, as on the last two I had either you Bob, or you Paul on previous rescues. That way I get the chance to see how each of you works. If these two are someone who has helped in the past, I'm fine with it, and your decisions. I know that this time our team is much smaller, but again as was stated earlier we are dealing with a more defined search area. So you can split up the other two who will be joining us however you would like."

"True, Jacob is the only one who hasn't teamed with you, and if we aren't able to find her, then we can ask to increase the amount of people helping with this effort." Paul replied.

"Oh, before I forget, be here at 5:00am tomorrow. I want us to be out there and searching by daylight or no later than 6:00am. I want to be sure that we do not waste a minute of daylight, since there is so little of it this time of year."

About this time their food arrived and for a while it was silent as all concentrated on what was before them. Then Bob asked. "Do you want to spend any additional time back at the firehouse this afternoon? I know you mentioned it. But looking over what we've covered this morning, plus what we've discussed here, and unless there is something else that is critical I think we've done all the planning we can."

"I've been thinking about that, but really since, as has been already stated a number of times, our area of searching is well defined. So I guess not." He looked briefly out through one of the windows and then continued. "It looks like it's snowing again and with this wind it is probably better if we go back and make sure our places are in good shape. Again I have to say what a vicious storm. I surely wouldn't want to be out in it. And when it finally blows itself out, I for one, will not be sorry to see it go." He then covered what they still needed to do before hitting the roads in the morning and got feedback from the rest and listening to their response he got agreement from the rest at the table. So after lunch they would break up and finish the preparations. After that there were some small talk and a little joking, and when finished, TD signed for the meals, and they broke up heading for their individual assignments and wouldn't meet again until Tuesday morning when they hoped the storm would be gone and they could begin the attempt to find the missing woman. Thinking back he remembered that he had asked many of the locals to donate some firewood, which they had. So he went to collect it and deliver it to the young widow. The last thing he and community wanted to see was for her and her 2 children to be cold. And once he was finished with that little chore he would head back to the firehouse and finish up the paperwork he had been working on. He suspected that he would be there long enough to pick up his children after school let out. So he added a brief stop there to inform the secretary of the schools to send a note out to the classes his children were in and have them walk down to the firehouse. And, while thinking about this, he decided that he would drop back in on Laura and she could meet the family there at the firehouse. Then they all could go home together. Laughing to himself he realized this meant that his daughter Sarah could ride with her mother home, and not be embarrassed by having to ride in the sheriff SUV.

Then thinking of Sarah he realized that probably this summer she would be getting her driver's license, and the complications that always brings, when the children begin to drive – more worries, more problems, and if she held to the contract that they had set up with all the children, a used car when she graduated. The contract was a simple one really. But it meant that the children would have to work in school. Not just float through and barely pass. To qualify they would have to maintain a "B" average or 3.0 GPA. Especially through high school as this was where too many distractions existed to keep their minds away from learning. Then again shaking his head he said to himself, "Sarah driving . . . wow, just where has the time gone?" He realized that it wouldn't be much longer and the other two children would be in a similar circumstance.

He pulled up behind the hardware store where the community put the donated firewood, got out, and then proceeded to load the back of the SUV. With the winds and blowing snow it was no picnic, but the building at least blocked the worst of it. In short order he finished, and glad to be back in the warm vehicle and out of that wind he drove over and delivered the additional wood. From there he stopped at the school, and the community center, before returning to the firehouse to continue his paperwork, and along the way to talk with dispatch to keep them up to date. With the small town quiet he was able to spend the rest of the day working on the paperwork, and before he realized it he heard, outside the firehouse, voices of children. At first because of his concentration he only heard them subconsciously, but eventually it penetrated and realized that his two boys were outside. That meant within an hour or so Sarah would be showing up. Then Terry and Robert came tearing into the office on some chase and catch game. With one glance they calmed down, and he asked. "So how was school today for the two of you?"

Both responded as he expected, "Ah it was school, what do you expect? Yeah it was okay."

When he had dropped off the note for the teachers to send his kids to the firehouse after school, he also found out if they had any homework, knowing that if possible they would try and avoid having anything to do with it. "Okay, you two I've set up this table here so you can do your homework. And don't tell me you don't have any, I've already have talked with your teachers and know better. So let's get to it and get it done before your sister and mother get here to join us."

"Ah dad, do we have to?" Robert asked, and then Terrance Jr. said, "Yeah, do we have to? I mean we are here at the firehouse and we would love to go climb a little on the fire trucks."

"Yes, I'm sure you would. But your responsibility comes first, and if you finish your work to my satisfaction and before the rest of the family arrives, *then,* I may allow you to get into one of the cabs and have a little fun . . . but only while I am there. There are too many things that can hurt you here or that you could damage. I've got some hot water going so you two can go into the kitchen here and make some hot cocoa. I have laid it out on the counter for you. So go do that and come back here and start your homework. I've got to continue on my paperwork. See, even as a grown up I have mine also." Smiling, he continued, "Now it isn't so bad. In a few years you will be done with your regular schooling and then go on to college. Your education is very important to your mother and me, even if it isn't to the two of you. Plus if you want to earn that car when you get out of school you have to keep your grades up. And skipping homework won't help you with that goal. Now go get your cocoa and then come back and get to work."

"Okay dad. Come on Robert let's go. Is there anything to eat, I'm hungry."

"Yeah me too." Robert chimed in.

Smiling and shaking his head TD said, "Yes, right next to the cups I've put something out for you." They then took off running for the kitchen both talking a mile a minute to each other. Thinking to himself he wondered if he was the same way as a child, especially on the food end. It seemed that the two boys were always hungry and it was like they needed two refrigerators just to keep enough food in the house just for them. Then yelling so they could hear him he said, "Be careful with that hot water. And clean up after yourselves. Remember I'll be checking up on you later."

He heard them mumble something and figured they had heard him. Now with them here there would be little more he would accomplish. As to keeping them to the task would be taking more of his time and concentration. It was time to get up and stretch anyway and go look over the plans for tomorrow just one more time, just to see if he had missed anything.

* * *

Bob, who was more the unofficial, official leader of the search and rescue, went across the street to the gas station. He needed to call the two who would be joining them tomorrow on the first part of the search. Of course if nothing were located tomorrow then the size of the force would increase tremendously. Adding a helicopter, and other equipment but for now it would just be the six of them. Both Art and Reggie were locals who also worked with him during the guide season. Both were seasoned outdoorsmen, single, and took the winters off to pursue whatever they pleased. The rest of the time they hired out as handymen, and of course, worked for him when his seasonal guide slash hiking business opened. Barely in their twenties and with no responsibilities other than themselves, yet because of growing up in the backcountry, showed a maturity well beyond their years, not that they didn't pull the pranks of their youth, but because living in such a place forces responsibility on you at a young age, they were very reliable. Each of the three teams would have a single trailer attached to one of the snowmobiles. In that trailer would be additional fuel for the machines, first aid kits, blankets and such. All the necessary stuff for a rescue – things like ropes and climbing equipment in case they had to repel down the side of a hillside or something to that effect.

The leader of each group would have the radio to keep in contact with the other groups. Plus a handi talkie between the team members, so if for some reason they got separated, they could keep in contact. The trailers or sleds that would attach to the back of the snowmobiles were kept at the firehouse and Paul would make sure that they were all prepared and ready. Sitting at his desk, after finishing the phone calls, and as Bob thought this, Paul pulled into the gas station to get the gas cans filled. He headed out the door and asked, "Paul, I was just thinking about you and putting the sleds together. Are they okay, and do you need some additional help?"

Paul, getting off the snowmobile pulling one of the sleds said, "No, not really. This is the last thing I have to do. They seem to be in pretty good shape from the last time we had to use them, so there really wasn't a lot that needed to be done other than inventory them. So if you can fill these cans and give me the receipt I'll get these loaded back at the firehouse and put the voucher on TD's desk so he can submit it and you can get paid. Then all we can hope is that this forecast is right and we can get out there and find this girl."

"On that subject what are your feelings here?" Bob asked

"As tough as this storm has been, experience tells me that there is little to none, as far as survival. Even for someone experienced, as this one has just been nasty from the start. But, funny thing, like TD I just sense that for some reason this one is different. At least I hope so. It is never a wonderful feeling when you find a body instead of a live person. Especially when you could see that they had been alive, had been fighting to stay that way, and finally end up dying. I hate that part. It's such a relief to find them living and to be able to reunite them with their families. But I guess even if they've died, at least it brings closure – not the outcome the families would want, but at least they then can put their loved one to rest and not be left wondering."

"Well, I hope the two of you are right. It has been my experience not to hope in cases such as this one. As you have stated this storm has been and still is nasty, and I think that I would be having trouble staying alive. I guess I'm just a realist here. I expect the worst but am hoping for the best. There, the cans are full. Come on let's get inside out of the wind where it is warmer and I'll get that voucher filled out."

"Sounds like a good idea to me. This wind just cuts right through you, and at times seems to take your breath away." They entered the gas station building and Paul continued, "Ah that's better. I can actually hear and I don't have to yell. So who are we bringing to this party anyway?"

"Art and Reggie – both have helped in the past, and of course as you know, have worked for me for a number of summers. They usually don't have a lot going during the winters so with their experience they were the logical choice."

"Well, you're not going to get me to argue. They are good, as long as they stay serious. Some of those pranks they have pulled in the past could have gotten someone hurt."

Laughing, as he thought about some of the pranks Bob said, "Funny you should mention that, as it was one of the things that had passed through my mind when I chose them. But I don't think it will be an issue in something like this. They are just a couple of fun loving barely in their twenties type of guys. Someday some woman will grab them and settle them down. But until then I think they are just enjoying life."

"I can't disagree. Okay then, got to get back and put this stuff in the trailers and tie everything down. See you in the morning around five at the café."

"Yeah and here's to the storm breaking tonight." And with that they said their good-byes and finished what they were doing.

Jacob headed home and assisted Caitlin on the chores left to do. There was no way that he would be leaving his wife to handle all the work in this weather. It also meant that he would have to be up extra early tomorrow to get most of the harder work accomplished so that what was left would not be a burden to Caitlin. "So how'd it go?" Caitlin asked.

"Okay, I guess. We are going to try to find a car that was probably involved with a single car traffic collision, a TC, and there was just one person driving, no passengers. With this storm I really don't hold out much hope, but I feel that we must do as much as we can. Who knows others have survived much worse." He then explained what he knew and they went from the barn where he had parked the snowmobile back into the warmth of the house, and the happy chatter of their two children. It was going to be a busy afternoon, and a very early morning.

Cathy – Monday Afternoon

What had awakened her anyway? She then realized that it must have been the cold. Since she wasn't moving anymore she was starting to feel the cold. Again thankful for finding this place she sat her backpack down in the semi darkness and dug out her flashlight. She wanted to study this little cave created by the dead trees. She still could hear the wind howling outside of this protected area and every once in a while a small bit of the breeze would penetrate her location causing her to shiver. She had to admit that it was very nice to both be out of the wind and to find a place where the snow had not reached. Looking around with the flashlight she saw that there was dead grass under her feet, while she couldn't stand completely up it was close. Then lying down and looking up she tried to see if she could look up through the top cover. But it was just a tangle of dead branches. As she continued to explore this small area she had found, she saw that there was plenty of dead wood lying everywhere close by. "Well, I guess if I needed a place that was like my car to get me out of this storm", she said out loud, "this is as close as I can get." At this point she continued talking with herself trying to keep her spirits up. "I wonder if I can maybe get a fire going here and not set the whole thing on fire." Truthfully not knowing the answer she sat down and began going through the backpack. She at least had that small camp stove, but was very worried that she was almost out of fuel. Of course, with her lack of experience, she had no real way of knowing.

She had always left the fire starting to the guys and really did not know if she could start a campfire anyway. Now, once again, ignorance could lead to her demise. "Let's think through this Cath' – how hard can it be?" Again she really didn't know. And once if she was successful could she keep it small enough to be safe? Her eyes had finally adjusted to the gloom of her sanctuary and she began to clear the ground to the bare earth somewhere towards one side of the space she had. She knew that it couldn't be too close to any of the dead trees as the heat could start all that wood on fire and then she would be in danger from the opposite, heat instead of cold. Thinking about it she shuddered, she didn't know which would be worse – dying from the cold or from a fire. Neither appealed to her, and she hoped that it would be neither. Next she gathered and piled as much of the dead wood that she could find in the area on the other side away from her future fire pit. Again knowing very little about fires she had no idea how much wood she would need. She knew that once the fire started the smoke created from the fire would have to go somewhere. She remembered that lesson from the fireplace at home. She remembered that for some reason the flue in the chimney had been closed and when one of the family members built a small fire the house immediately filled with smoke. And they had to open all the windows and doors to get the smoke out of the house. Then for the longest time everything smelled of smoke.

Trying to judge where the smoke would go once she got the fire going she took one of the longer dead branches and pushed it up through the tangle that was her roof. After some effort she finally was able to work the branch most of the way through and hoped that it was enough. Then, as she tried to pull her tool back inside, it hung up on something. No matter how she pulled down on it, it wouldn't budge. Running out of patience she worked it up and down and twisted it around until whatever it had hung up on, freed and it came loose suddenly putting her on her rear end with a thud, and pain. "Ouch, that hurt!" Then getting up on her knees as she rubbed her bottom she continued, "I really thought I had enough padding back there, but I guess not. Wonder if I bruised something other than my pride?" She realized that she had been lucky in another way. She had really been jerking on that limb and had put most of her weight and strength in that last pull that had freed the limb. She could have struck herself with that branch and might have been stabbed with the broken end making a really nasty wound. Once again her emotions and impatience had almost put her into a more serious situation. *I've really got to learn to control my anger, and, of course, learn more patience. How many times have I been told that?* She had to admit that it had been many times over her life, and not only from her parents. *I guess if nothing else I am having many of my weaknesses, things that I really need to work on, shown me.* It hurt, and it was humbling. At least there were no others around to see her learn these hard lessons. Yet, she had to admit that right now she didn't care. She would love to have someone else right there with her. She was a people person, and this solitude that she had been living was almost too much.

In the twilight created by the deadfall she was in she found that even when her eyes had adjusted to the gloom that it was still difficult to see anything. The area she was in was very uneven, and to find any level ground within her small space seemed impossible. As she explored this space she found that large tree trunks bounded three sides. The side she had entered from was created from the branches of two of those trees. On top of these fallen giants lay others in a haphazard manner. When she had probed the area above her to see if it was open somewhere to the air and then got her branch stuck, she showered herself and the surrounding area with a little snow. It was cold! Now that she knew that there could be a fire, she needed to prepare the area she had selected, making it safer for her planned fire. Looking into the backpack she found the sheathed survival knife that was part of the kit and started digging with the point trying to get out some of the rocks that seemed to be buried in the hard frozen soil, wanting to build a ring with them. She didn't know why, but it always seemed that was the way it was done. Now that she had found such a place as this, *this small shelter*, she did not want to lose it to carelessness. So she worked slowly and with effort on building a safe small pit for her fire. Outside she could hear the winds and every once in a while a little breeze would find its way into where she was. After what seemed like an eternity she was ready to try her luck at building a fire. She remembered her father telling both she and her brother about fire building. Again because it was something she felt she would never use, so she really did not listen very closely.

"Okay Cath', what did he say?" Rubbing her eyes and her forehead she thought a few minutes, and then remembered that in the emergency kit there were some fire starters he had included. They were homemade and consisted of candle wax, sawdust and a wick. The mixture when hot had been placed in a cardboard egg carton and then once it had hardened cut up into individual pieces. She thought that there might have been six of them included. She then dug into the pack and found one of them and placed it in the middle of her small pit and then carefully placed small dry twigs close to it. She then made sure that she had plenty of wood in different sizes close by. So that when the fire started she could slowly feed it until it would handle the larger wood. She then lit the fire starter and as the wick burned down it started consuming the mixture of wax and sawdust. At this point she started adding the twigs. Expecting them to burn immediately she was surprised when all they did was smoke, glow red, and then become ash. *Why don't they catch fire? After all, all of this stuff is dead, so why doesn't it burn?* Trying again she ended with the same result. It seemed so easy when daddy had done it. What was she doing wrong? She then grabbed some of the dead grass she had cleared and put that on top of the fire starter. Immediately it began to smoke heavily, briefly filling her space with the smoke making her cough, followed by the grass making large crackling sounds, and at first like the twigs did not burn. Then the heavy smoke cleared and the grass caught fire and burned rapidly. In a panic now she started adding small pieces of wood and found that like the grass they would smoke, but eventually began burning. Again, what was the reason for this stuff not to just burn? The next thing she noticed, after the smoke from the grass had cleared was that her area was filling with some of the smoke, forming a layer above her head. Now why wasn't it going out? She began to cough as she inhaled some of the acrid light blue smoke. With what little that were burning and the amount of smoke coming off of the tiny fire there was little heat. *Why is this so difficult?* She then heard a hissing noise coming from the wood as some of it burned. It sort of reminded her of a heating teapot before it started whistling. Could it be that this wood was damp or wet? Thinking about it she realized that most likely it was. After all it was winter, and winter is wet. It was something she had never considered, like so many others things that were now being revealed to her. Why hadn't she paid closer attention to what daddy had tried to pass on to her? If she had, some of this probably would be easier.

Now, with care, she found that she had a small fire going, and she began to feed it. She found that anything she added would steam before finally burning. Then she noticed that slowly there appeared to be some tiny red-hot coals building up on the bottom, and it was these that seemed to give off most of the heat. Slowly as the fire became hotter it began to form a draft and the smoke started filtering out the top and out of her shelter. At this point it began to draw the layer of smoke that was in her shelter out with it. She decided to bring the wood she had gathered closer to the fire, so that it would dry out from the heat, making it easier to burn. Because of her concentration on getting the fire going and making sure where she was would remain a safe place, she had paid little attention to her own personal needs. At this point she realized that her feet, shoes, and socks were soaked and her feet were quite cold – maybe dangerously so. Well she had a fire going now, so she removed the shoes and socks and placed them near the fire, on a makeshift rack she had made from her firewood, so that they could dry out. She had to admit that putting her feet towards the fire felt really, really nice, although her feet stung initially from the heat. This told her that she had been close to freezing them. While her feet warmed, she realized that with this small fire her space was slowly warming a little. Then she noticed that her pants were wet from about the knees down. She had more than one pair on. So taking off the outer ones she draped them over one of the many branches and then moved closer to the fire to dry out the ones she kept on. The fire cheered her a little. And the flickering light and heat made it almost comfortable. Something about a fire just seemed to make everything seem better. Listening, it was easy to tell that the winds were blowing hard and she suspected that it was snowing again. She felt very fortunate to have found this place. At that moment she realized that her path she had broken to get here, that obvious trail in the snow she had left would be destroyed. Anyone out looking for her would have no clue as to which way she went. The note she had written had been brief and had left the impression that she would be heading back the way she came by the road. It had been her plan, but she had never found the road. And she really had no idea where she was or even if she was close to that road. She truly was on her own, by herself, and as far as she knew no one was even close to her present location. When she fully realized this it added additional fear. She was finding that as time continued that keeping her emotions in control was becoming more and more difficult. Yet at the same time she realized that if she didn't, and panic took over, it would be over for her. She would be dead, simple and true.

Now, in her new location – where this was – she once again had to wait out this part of the storm. At least where she was she was sheltered. She hoped that that it would keep that pack from roaming also. She really had not gotten as far away from them as she would have liked. But then thought that at least her scent would have been obliterated by what was happening right now. At least she wouldn't run out of wood as she was surrounded by it. Again the fire almost made it cheery. In almost any other circumstance it probably would have. Relaxed she dug in the emergency backpack to see what was left and in one of the smaller pockets she felt what seemed to be a small book. Thinking to herself she asked. *What is this? And how did I ever miss it? Probably just another survival book daddy placed here.* Then pulling it out she immediately realized that daddy had not placed it there but mom. Rubber banded around it was a note from her stating, "While the book your dad provided helps with your physical survival, this one is for your spiritual survival. You need to have both working for you. If you have found this it means that you are in a bad situation right now. Reading this New Testament and praying to God for help can comfort you and give you the necessary strength to carry on until the situation is resolved. Remember God is always there. And remember we both love you deeply – mom." This immediately brought the tears back. Even momma had been in on this backpack, and their love for her could not be denied. One thing for sure she wasn't going anywhere soon, and her choice of reading materials very limited. What would it hurt to at least read something out of it to pass the time? She knew that it would be a short read at this time, since she was weary – exhausted really. The hike to here, wherever here was, had completely burned what energy she had and she could feel the weight of fatigue through her entire being. So where should she start her reading? Good question. "I guess just start at the beginning." And why not, it had been a while since she had even opened a Bible, any Bible at all. Slowly the tears subsided and as she attempted to find both a place that was somewhat comfortable and still get the flickering light from the warming soft fire so she could see the pages. She still had plenty of water and a few of the energy bars left. So while she began to read she ate one of the bars and washed it down with water.

Hillstown – Late Monday Afternoon

It was snowing again and the winds were howling. It was a time to be indoors looking out at the storm and not be in it. With the family together at the firehouse TD called the café to see if there was a chance they could pick up something instead of having to go home and fix it from scratch. But disappointed he found that they were already closed. "Oh well Laura . . . I was hoping. Guess we'll head home and with all of us helping, we probably can whip out something pretty quickly." Then turning to the boys he said, "Now remember I want your chores taken care of as soon as you have changed out of your school clothes. The dogs need their care and will get it before we eat tonight. Then you can help your sister with the horses out in the barn. I suspect about that time dinner will be ready and you also should be done. So let's go."

"And I second what your dad just told you. He and I will work on getting the food on the table, and Sarah, I want to see how your homework is coming also. Your dad made the boys do theirs here, but there wasn't time by the time you and I arrived. Yes I know you've done well, and have maintained your part of our contract. But I am the mom, and it is my responsibility to be sure that everything is being done that can be." They, as a family, headed out, and in a small caravan headed home, knowing how traitorous the roads would be.

* * *

Bob, once everything had been wrapped up at the gas station, headed home. He wanted to make sure that the pack he carried with him on these search and rescues was complete. He didn't remember if he had checked it since the last time it had been used. As far as the personnel going tomorrow that was complete. Everyone would be at the café tomorrow morning at 5:00am even if the storm hadn't quit. The forecast still showed that it was blowing itself out and would be gone by tomorrow. As he pulled into the yard he had a few chores to do, including taking care of the animals he used in his guide business. It would be a few hours before he would be able to get into the house and get his own meal. But he had to admit that working with his animals relaxed him. And even if there wasn't a woman in his life he got much of the companionship from the animals, as they were always eager to see him – even if it was, because they knew that he was about to feed them, or groom them, or put some attention their way. As he entered the barn he could see that the hay was getting low. He would need to order another ton of the stuff, another reason for the storm to end. There would be no way for it to be delivered until it did. At least the grain he fed the animals was still in good supply.

Looking out where the animals entered the barn area he saw that their water trough was icing over. "That's not good." He told himself. He grabbed a hammer from the toolbox and broke up the ice, grabbing and dumping it on the ground. "Damn, that's cold!" He said out loud. Then blowing on his fingers and hands to help get them warm he stuck them in his pockets. Then looking out into the pen area where the animals were he noticed that once it warmed up and the snow and ice started melting that this area was going to be a muddy mess. Well, before it got too bad he would turn the stock out into the larger meadow area. But before he did that he would need to walk it to see if the fence needed any repairs. The last thing he wanted to do was to chase his stock all over creation if they got out. *Well, I guess I've got a lot of work ahead of me here. Sometimes it's just difficult to find the time to run both the businesses and what needs to be taken care of here.* Shaking his head he worked what he needed to do with the animals and then entered his cold house. The first thing he needed to do here was build a fire and get the chill out and then he could fix a meal, relax a little, followed by putting what he needed into his car so that it wouldn't be accidentally left behind.

* * *

Jacob had the dairy farm to work before night, which meant feeding and milking the cows, making sure that the stalls were clean, and the equipment used was sterile. Once milked the cows would be turned out into a pasture, which also had a large barn for shelter. He would follow this up by making sure that the processing equipment did its job. When the milk and cream was pasteurized, and placed into the large refrigerated tanks he could finally call it and head in. Again, this storm didn't make the process any easier. He was quite happy about the equipment. If he would have had to milk the cows by hand, as it used to be done, then he would have been out there well past dark. Then, like tomorrow, would have been up well before sunrise to start the process all over again. Once the cattle were fed, milked and turned back out, Caitlin and the two children would join him to finish the cleanup. As a family they would head back in, at which time Caitlin would begin dinner and he would give the two children their baths. While this was happening he could always smell the wonderful smells wafting from the kitchen. It always made his mouth water in anticipation.

They then would pray and eat dinner, followed by a family devotional and Bible reading. All this happening before turning on the TV for a short time, and once the clock on the wall reached nine, sending the children off to bed. They would follow this by spending some quiet and quality time together before heading off to bed themselves. As always, there were a few chores that had to be done, once the children were in bed, and in these they both shared the responsibility. Once they finally got to bed very rarely did they have a problem falling asleep. They worked hard, and when the day was over they were tired. For him the day would begin at 3:30am on Tuesday. So that he could get most of the morning work completed before he needed to show up at the café at 5:00am.

* * *

Paul, when he finished working on the trailers that were located in the storage shed at the firehouse, headed home. He had much to think about. What was it that put one in such circumstances anyway? With the rescues he had been involved with over the years – some successful and some not – what was it that determined if someone would live or die? He, being a member of the volunteer fire department, had responded to many TC's over the years. Many were very messy, since they only had a two-lane blacktop road in the area. At times someone would get impatient and attempt to pass a slower vehicle only the crash head on into one coming from the other direction. Many a time he could see that a second or even a half of a second could have meant the difference between a crash or avoiding it completely. It was almost enough for him to believe in fate. After all, if some of the past victims had left their starting points even a second earlier or later then nothing would have happened to them. A second was truthfully a very short period of time. Yet that brief period of time seemed to make a difference in these people's lives. It almost made one second-guess everything one did. He saw much the same thing with the ones who became lost in the forest.

"Oh well," He said softly, "Guess I'm not going to solve the world's problems trying to figure this one out." He then realized that as he was heading home that he had been thinking about this more than paying attention to his driving. Before he realized it he was pulling up to his small log cabin. He could hear his dog Beau, a chocolate lab, barking eagerly, and happily. Smiling he thought, "At least I have someone who really cares for me." He got out of the car and headed around the back where Beau was kept. Seeing he all excited and full of joy from seeing his master pushed all those thoughts he had right out of his head. He let the dog out of his pen that Beau had to stay in while Paul was away, and Beau took off full of energy and joy disappearing in and out of the falling snow. This brought another smile to his face as the dog wanting to play enticed Paul to join him for a short while. Finally winded from the chase and play he called it quits and headed inside. He needed to build a fire and get dinner going. Unfortunately Beau would have to be in his pen all day tomorrow, so for now he let him run. Eventually he would be let into the cabin and spend the evening there.

Where his cabin was located kept it out of most of the strong winds; it had been built close to and against a hillside, which provided the wind block. Whoever had originally planned and built this cabin had planned well. As far as he knew he was the fourth or fifth owner. So the original builder had faded with time. The cabin sat on five acres that were mostly wooded. He was far enough away from neighbors and roads that he rarely heard anything. And it was one of the things that had drawn him here in the first place. Not needing much, he was living on a small inheritance from his parents whom had died years ago. He worked odd jobs in the area, and pursued his passion. He loved to track, and being an amateur photographer took many a scenic or animal photo that he would sell through his on-line store. So far he had little to complain about and loved being single at this time in his life.

These thoughts brought him full circle and his mind back to the present problem. Could they, would they find this missing woman? For all they knew she had gotten further than they had thought and this search could end up being a wild goose chase from their end. Well, until they actually searched it out tomorrow that question couldn't be answered. So why worry? Why? *Because,* simply stated, it was his nature. Yes he fronted as someone who cared little and enjoyed company and life, but that was only one of his many roles he presented to the world at large. He fed the dog and the food he was preparing for himself started permeating the cabin and made his mouth water. He suddenly realized that he was very hungry and the smells from the cooking food didn't help.

Cathy – Monday Evening

Before she had gotten very far into the New Testament, she found that she could barely keep her eyes open. So giving up for now she put it down and put some additional wood on the fire. Then trying to find a place close to it so that she could keep warm she laid down using the backpack as a pillow and covered herself with the emergency blanket. She still could hear the howling of the wind, and knew that once again, it was snowing, but right now these things seemed to be unimportant as she faded from consciousness to almost immediate deep sleep. How long she slept she really didn't know. But it was the cold that once again awakened her. When she opened her eyes it was to darkness. So she knew that at least it was nighttime now. She could see a slight glow from some of the remaining coals of her fire. Shaking from the cold she nursed those coals with a bit of her dry kindling back to life and shortly had a fire burning once more. Again she could hear the storm raging outside of her shelter and she really wondered how it was that she had found this place at all. She knew that if she hadn't that it wouldn't have mattered at this time, as she would have died out there. It was a very sobering thought for her to realize how close to death she had been. And to be honest, still was.

The flickering yellow light from the fire cast shadows that danced with the flames and mesmerized her, almost causing her to fall back to sleep, now that it was warming up in her small space once again. But she was noticing that once again her bladder ached so it was time to go fill that cup again. She had to admit that by this time she had become quite expert at it, and figured that the next time she had to fill one of those small cups at the doctor's office that it was be no problem at all – well maybe. That was of course if she survived what she was presently going through. There still were no guarantees of that at all. So far she had, yes so far she had, but just because it had been so, left her with no illusions as to what her future might be. She was lost now, and in the middle of a snowstorm that seemed bent on her destruction, or so it appeared. Once again she began wondering if she had just stayed with her car would things have turned out better for her. It really was too late – much too late – to go down that road in her mind. She hadn't remained and she was here. So now totally committed to these actions, she remembered one of the things her dad used to tell her about that. He would say that, "Once you have committed yourself to something, most of the time there is no retreating from your course. You can then 'what if' yourself to death thinking about other ways. But in the end all your 'what ifing' means nothing and the worry created leads to useless waste of your time and energy." He was right. She could not go back and change what she had done. So worrying about what might have been was just a waste. She suspected that once again she had allowed her impatience to get in the way of her reason and that was why she was here right now.

At least until daylight she was here, and maybe longer. She thought that there would be little chance of finding another place, such as this, somewhere ahead of her. Without thinking about it she picked up the New Testament and began reading it in the dim flickering light of her little fire. Suddenly she realized that it was like talking to an old friend that she hadn't seen in years, which was in fact the truth, as it had been years since she had opened any Bible. When she had begun reading the New Testament from the beginning the familiar Christmas story was there. Then she remembered the little phrase to help her remember the order of books in the New Testament, which had entered her mind unbidden. "Matthew, Mark, Luke, and John, saddle a horse and

I'll jump on." She remembered learning that somewhere in Sunday school. And then there was AWANA's; she remembered spending Wednesday nights as part of that group. Her mind began drifting back to those times, and the many discussions and prayers they had as a family, then for whatever reason she had pulled away and had decided that this faith was no longer for her. After all, what good was something like this that was created back in ancient history? It had no relevance for today's world. Yet she saw that both her parents, with Keith and his parents, remaining strong and true to Christ and God. She knew that she and Keith had many discussions and disagreements on the subject – both of them strong on their side of the argument. At times she had to admit to herself that his points and facts were getting to her. But while she would silently see the point, she and her pride would not let it be seen by Keith. Many times she would simply change the subject and let it alone for a while before they would begin their *discussions* again.

This brought her back to this little book she was holding. What was it about this thing that held so much power? The ones who study it say it has the power of God. But how could that be? Here she went again, in that circle of thought that always was there when someone made that statement. Again, how could a creator who had created the vast universe care for this minor spec of nothing, let alone her? It made absolutely no sense at all. Still, she had to admit to herself that during this present situation that had more than once brought her close to death, she had reached out to . . . to . . . well to what she really didn't know . . . a higher intelligence? Yes she had to admit that she had asked God to help her – was he actually doing that? So far she was still alive and knew that because of her lack of experience in surviving something like this that maybe, just maybe, that was exactly what was happening. One thing for sure, she was finding herself questioning her very faith and why she had rejected God and Christ. One thing for sure, they were not welcome in the college she had attended. She could see that many who claimed to be Christians were belittled, harassed, and generally looked down upon as something less, and joked about openly. Most of the professors considered such things as religion as a joke, something for the primitive people, something to explain away things they did not understand. And since she had been leaning that way anyway, it was easy to fall into line with this thinking.

But now she was beginning to have some doubts. Either she was incredibly lucky or something else was happening here. But at this moment she wasn't quite ready to change her views, or her mind for that matter. For now she would just rack it up to luck. *Yes for now, but . . . yeah I know, no if, ands, or buts allowed.* Then she wondered why she was fighting this so hard? After all both families, hers and Keith's were strong Christians. She was the only one who had rejected what they had accepted, what was with that anyway? Honestly she had no answer to that one. Turning back to that little book she began reading again. As she read, in her mind verses started coming back to her, ones that she had learned years ago, in those Sunday school classes. To see if she had remembered them accurately she started flipping through the book and found that she still remembered how the books were laid out. This was a surprise as it had been, what, at least 10 years and probably more since she had even opened a Bible. For the first time, other than those desperate moments in her near past, she prayed. "Lord, I am trying hard to understand what is happening here. I don't yet know if you are real, as it says here in the Bible. Yet I know that my family and my fiancé believe in you as a personal God. It is so much to accept and understand, and I do not know where this is leading or where I am going. Can you help me understand and to come to terms with what's happening to me now, and what my future is?" Then running out of thoughts and words there was a silence and then she said, "Oh yeah, amen." In one sense she felt a little foolish, and in another, quite relieved.

At this point she really did not know how she stood as of yet. If she lived through this, then she might have the opportunity to really go over everything and understand more. But for now there was just too much happening for her to think straight. And once again, with the hypnotic flickering of her small fire, she found she had been staring out at nothing and once again she was starting to drift off. Before this happened she put everything away and rechecked her supply of wood. She followed this by placing a rather large piece on the fire so that it would last quite a while. She also piled off the edge smaller pieces that would fall into the fire as the night progressed. She hoped that doing it this way would mean she would still have some hot coals to keep her fire going and not have to start all over again. Then taking care of her physical needs once again she tried to find a comfortable position close to the fire and while lying there stared into her small comforting fire, with this being the last thing she remembered as she fell to sleep once again.

Hillstown Rescue – Tuesday Morning

It was 4:30 in the morning when TD headed out the door to drive over to the café. Somewhere, just a short time earlier the storm had left, leaving the world bathed in the light of a full moon. Looking around all he could see was an unbelievably beautiful winter wonderland. He half expected the white witch from the Narnia books to arrive in her sleigh and ask what was he doing here. After the winds had quieted, to hear his footsteps crunching in the snow was a surprise. In fact it seemed to be dead calm. He even could see his breath coming out in clouds, and breathing the air he knew that it was quite cold, maybe dangerously so. He suspected that the storm probably had dropped somewhere between one and two feet of snow on the ground. But it was hard to tell with the winds that had accompanied the storm. Now there were areas where it was much deeper, being caused by winds as the snow was piled into drifts. Well one good thing would be coming out of this. The storm was done and the sun should be out today making their job a little easier. But as far as warmth from that sun he really suspected that it would be little to none. Still with the sun out it would make things seem a little more positive. He got into the SUV and carefully drove over to the café. Where, as he approached, he could see the lights were on and when his headlights brushed past the front of the building he saw the rest of the team standing there waiting on his arrival and at the same time waiting for 5:00am so that they could enter. Parking the vehicle a little more carefully than the last visit he got out and joined the team. Before he could say anything, Faith was at the door and yelled, "Well, just don't stand there, come inside where it's warm. Your food is ready and I've put some tables together so that you all can be together." Then beckoning them in they all followed her and then got a whiff of hot coffee and the smell of pancakes and bacon – such a warm comforting smell in the mornings.

After sitting down TD looked at the team, and most were blurry eyed and barely awake except Jacob. He suspected that Jacob had been up for a couple of hours taking care of the farm so that most of the work would not fall to Caitlin. Most likely the fatigue would hit him later in the day, but for now he was the most wide-awake member. "Jacob, tell me, I know that you've been up for a couple of hours, was the storm gone when you got up?" TD asked.

"Not quite, I mean it wasn't blowing or snowing. But there was still clouds obscuring the moon. But as I worked they became broken and the full moon would show through, and then before I left to come here it was quite clear and calm, beautiful truthfully."

"Oh by the way guys where did you park your snowmobiles? The one I am using", TD said, "is down at the firehouse, you know, the one that is owned by the county, as I can't afford one of my own."

"They're over at the gas station right now." Bob replied. "Just before we leave they'll be filled up. Then any gas needed after that will be charged to the county as part of the effort."

"Thought that might be the case, but wasn't sure. As sometimes you guys have the equipment here or somewhere else. Just wanted to know what our starting point was to be."

About this time Faith started serving them, and from that point eating was a serious business so not much was said until they had finished the meal. Then sitting there and drinking coffee TD turned to Faith and asked, "Can you fill the thermoses so at least with the lunches you packed we can have something hot out there?"

"Already ahead of you there . . . Just don't have your thermos as of yet."

"Yeah, that's true, I left it in the truck out there in the cold so will have to go get it. Okay guys it looks like it is getting close to 6:00am, so let's meet at the firehouse and get this search started. I am hoping and praying that when this particular chapter is over that we are successful in what we are trying to do today." Then getting up he headed out to the SUV, retrieved the thermos and returned to the café. As he re-entered the team had picked up their lunches and thermoses and was heading out the door. "See you all shortly." He said, and then handed his thermos to Faith who handed it to Ron. While Ron was taking care of the thermos she handed him the invoice to sign so that she could submit it and get paid. After looking it over and signing it he said, "Thanks Faith, I know that at times I ask a lot of you and Ron. But I really feel the need to get the team moving as early as we can and that means imposing on you." In the background he could hear the snowmobiles starting and moving out.

"Don't think anything of it TD. It helps our business and any additional time you and your team can put in to help save someone means only a little loss of sleep for us." She handed him his thermos and said. "Okay here's your coffee, and I heard them too. So you better get going, it's going to be light enough to see in a short time. And good luck on this. I really hope you find that young woman alive. She really had been excited with the prospect of seeing her fiancé, and it would be sad to have it end so tragically."

"Thanks again Faith, and I agree. I would rather find them *alive*, than deceased . . . Anyway got to go." He headed out the door, got into the SUV, and drove over to the firehouse where the rest of the team was waiting for him. Parking the vehicle in his spot, he got out, hearing the end of a statement, from whom he did not know, but it brought a laugh from the group.

". . . always late, probably was late to his own wedding."

"Now that isn't true, I was early." TD responded.

"Yeah I suspect it had to do with something about a shotgun", which again, brought laughter to the group. "Just kidding", Paul said. "After all we didn't even know you back then. I suspect you chased your wife until she caught you. I know that's generally how it works." Stretching and then yawning Paul continued. "Looks like its light enough to do this. Are you ready? I have a feeling that even though there will be sunlight today it's not going to be warm at all."

Starting his snowmobile, which decided to be stubborn followed by checking the hitch, as his was one of the units with the sled attached, he climbed on and said, "Let's do this, and may we be very successful. As you know we all are going to work this first 10 to 15 miles. Jacob and I will work the road, Bob you and your team member will work the north side, Paul you and your team member will work the south side. I know that it will be easier for Jacob and me, but we will not be pushing it, as we will be looking for damage to the railings and such, or to the trees. Once we reach the end of the first search area, then we will break down into the smaller teams and work the different stretches that have been assigned. Keep in radio contact." He then signaled them to head out and then led the way to the east on SR44.

As they arrived at the road the sun began to rise above the horizon shining directly into their eyes. Even with the eye protection the sun reflecting off the snow was bright – almost blinding. It made it almost impossible to even see any features ahead of them let alone the road. Slowing to a stop on the edge of town he signaled the team to break and begin their search areas, Bob to the north and Paul to the south. He saw the two younger members showing some of their youthful vigor and was showing off their skills with the snowmobiles. He knew that this would only be a brief display and that they would become very serious about their job shortly. Squinting through the bright sunlight he could see the road track ahead of him only as a straight flat line in the snow. Plus, now and then, one of the side rails would be above the snow, or one of the many highway signs would put in an appearance. "Jacob, take the west bound lane and stay somewhat close to the shoulder so that you have a better chance of catching any damage done to the railing or to some of the trees. I suspect with what we have received out of this storm that will be the only hints we will get. Of course I'll be doing the same thing here in the east lane. Also keep an eye out for the ones there to the north of you. I'm doing the same with the ones to the south. We don't want to get too far ahead of them since ours is the easier path for now."

"Makes sense TD. Do you really think it actually happened this close in? I know we discussed it back at the firehouse, but I figure if she did crash this close in that she would have come back into town if she had been able."

"Most likely this will be a waste of time, but we just can't take that kind of chance. Everything that I have gathered on this woman says she knows nothing about surviving in the backcountry. So if she crashed close in, who's to say that she didn't get herself turned around and tried to head back to town only to be going in the opposite direction. It's something that even happens to the most experienced every once in a while." Pausing for a moment and smiling he continued, "Which I know is embarrassing but it's the reality of it. So we just cannot take a chance." Taking a deep breath and looking around once more he said. "Okay we've sat here enough. The sun is up enough that we aren't looking directly into it and maybe things will be a little more visible now." With that he led off and they began the close and slow search along the roadway, as the other four members searched off the road to either side. In a way he was thankful for the snow as it made it somewhat easier for the ones off the road to move.

After about an hour of close intense searching he called a halt and had the team come in at his location. He figured that they had covered close or all of the distance at this point and after the break they would move on to their assigned areas to move this search along. As he waited he dismounted the snowmobile and went back to the trailer he was towing. It was time for some coffee and yes it was cold, very cold, and that hot coffee would hit the spot. While welcome, the sun carried very little heat and in fact it felt like the temperatures still had to be close to zero degrees, if not below zero. He hoped that as the day progressed that it would warm up at least a little. Even as bundled as he was he could feel the chill penetrate right through his clothing. They had kept in radio contact during the hour plus, throughout the area they had been searching, and there was no hint of anything out of the normal. So, as originally thought, the TC had to happen further out. Yet until they had searched this area they couldn't eliminate it. Again by having everyone involved as they had been, they were able to get the whole area eliminated in short order. Pulling a large thermos from the trailer he saw Bob and Reggie approaching with Reggie pulling one last stunt of gunning the snowmobile up the embankment and jumping the unit up onto the road completely clearing the road, flying briefly into the air before settling back on the surface. He could see a large grin on his face. All he could do was shake his head. These kids could do things with these machines that he never thought could be possible.

Paul, with Art then came from the east and joined them there. Stopping and shutting the snowmobiles down they refilled the tanks grabbed a cup of coffee and generally tried to warm up. Paul saying, "At least the conditions are favorable, but damn, it's cold. I for one am glad we brought a lot of coffee. I do hope it will be enough . . . anyway, nothing of importance or unusual to report. Other than the tracks we are making it all appears to be virgin snow. Haven't even seen a rabbit track out there – although I suspect that will change shortly with the clearing of the skies. Art ranged pretty far out just in case and overall for us it was easy going. I know it will change ahead of us but I for one am glad for the easy start. Just wish we could have ended it here. But I guess it's rarely this easy."

"I think that this will bring out the skiers once the roads are cleared. You know one last ski run before the snow begins to melt. I suspect that this weekend will be a very busy one for all of us. After all, this probably added a couple of feet of new powder to the slopes. And the storm stopped just about the right time to allow the roads to be open. Don't think you're going to get much rest this weekend TD." Bob said, "These flatlanders will keep you on your toes."

"I am sure that you are right. And if we are unsuccessful here, then with that many eyes on the road one of them might just spot our missing vehicle. Okay, guys I don't want it to come down to someone this weekend finding our missing person. I want it to be today. Paul you have the furthest distance to go for your search area so when you and Art are ready go ahead and head out. As the sun starts to set I want all of us to meet right here. I've tied some flagging here to this sign to mark it. Jacob and I have the next furthest area to search and Bob you and Reggie have the area from this point out to our starting point. Let's get to this, as our daylight will be gone before we know it. Keep in radio contact both with me, and with your partner. I expect an update hourly. I know that in much of this area you and your partner will be out of sight of the other. And yes I know I say it every time, but it bares a reminder. I don't want to have to come looking for any one of you. Oh one last thing, if any one of you does find something make sure it isn't one of the wrecks that hasn't been pulled out as of yet, as there are a few still around from some of the accidents that happened this winter. I've tried to mark them on your maps, but I am not sure if all of them are there. Of course be sure to check them out just in case this one ended crashing in the same area – wouldn't be the first time. Good luck and good hunting." The distances assigned ranged with Bob and Reggie having the most area to cover since they could start immediately searching, while each outlying area would be smaller. They restarted the snowmobiles, after finishing their coffee, and headed out, there was much work and searching ahead of them, and possibly someone alive and injured, desperately needing immediate help, and waiting to be found.

As the other two teams pulled away from them Reggie turned to Bob and asked, "So how do you want to tackle this? I am sure the other two teams will take a quick look as they head for their areas they plan on searching."

"Been thinking about that. And that was quite some stunt you pulled coming up to the road that way."

Laughing Reggie replied, "No big deal, it's something we do all the time. Of course, every once in a while, like all things, we get it wrong and then it can really hurt."

"Yeah, I bet. We are supposed to meet back here at the end of the day so my thought is to work the actual road out to the end of our search area and then go over the sides and work those areas back to here. How does that sound to you?"

"Hey you're the boss on this. I'm just here to help. No prob' at all for me. Shall we then?"

Nodding, Bob replied, "Yeah no . . . what did you say, prob' at all. I'll work the left side here and you can work the right. It's not necessary we stay together, as you know, just somewhat close." With that they headed out working the road, being careful to do a thorough search along the edge and embankments of the road. On his side of the road lay a drop off of about 60 feet while on Reggie's side was an embankment. So Reggie was quickly out of sight as there was very little for him to search at this point. Later as they climbed and wound through the mountains the roles would be reversed. Looking carefully for any damage to the rails on the road edge where they were not buried in the new snow, and to some of the treetops that came to about the height of the road he crept along. With this fresh snow things would not be easy. Any damage would now be days old and subtle. Sometimes the light had to be just right to show any changes. A couple of times he got off the snowmobile to take a closer look only to come up empty. It was definitely a cold day and as well as he was dressed for the weather; at times it would penetrate all the way through.

* * *

The rest of the group continued up the road four strong, all searching as they went. Because of the short days of winter's end they could not take extra time to do a thorough search as they traveled . . . Only enough time to see if something seemed wrong or different, something that would really stand out. Like Bob and Reggie, when they reached their assigned areas then they would begin to really search. They pulled up on mile marker 56 and here TD and Jacob dropped out to begin their searching in earnest as Paul and Art continued on further up the road. Bob and Reggie had twelve miles to cover, while TD and Jacob had eight, and that left five for Paul and Art. If there had been more daylight the plan would have been to cover much more distance and area. It worked out to about twenty five miles for Tuesday, and if nothing were found then on Wednesday they would cover an equal amount of area further out. Still, the hope was that they would be successful today on all fronts. They would find the TC, they would find the woman alive, and there would be happiness from the families, and relief from the searchers.

Like Bob and Reggie, TD and Jacob decided to start by searching the road and then proceed back working the edges. It seemed to be the most logical as the vehicle would have to have left this road at some point, and where it did it was hoped that there would be some evidence. So to follow generally the same route as the woman had traveled just made sense to them. If, by the end of their area with nothing obvious found, then the search over the side, which would be more difficult and intensive, would become necessary. At the beginning of their search area the road cut through one of the mountains leaving slopes rising up from the roadway as the road slowly climbed towards the top of one of the minor peaks. Here there was a series of "S" curves, and the road was wide at this location, with an area to pull off and put on chains, if necessary. Plus the westbound lane had a pull out area for trucks to test brakes before descending into the valley below this point. Here the winds were stronger and definitely had a sting to them. Any exposed skin felt as if it was frozen immediately. There seemed to be small ice crystals with the wind and when they struck uncovered skin it hurt.

Temporarily finding a place out of the wind they took a quick break. TD called Bob on the radio to inform him that they had reached their starting point and if they had found anything. Bob had replied that so far they had come up empty. Too bad really, as this meant that they would have to continue . . . no easy way out of this one. TD knew when Paul and Art reached their starting point that they would check in. Then every hour on the hour they would continue to check in with each other until either the TC was located or they ran out of time for this day. Checking his watch he saw that it was pushing 10:00 am, which meant they would have about six to seven hours of search time left before the sun set and it became too dark to be able to continue. "God, Lord above, let us be fortunate in our search and may we find this missing woman alive and well. Yet, in all things it is your will and direction and plan that we must understand and follow. Thank you Lord for hearing my prayer, amen", TD whispered under his breath. "Okay Jacob which side do you want? It doesn't matter to me."

"Okay, because I am left handed it means that I probably would do better looking over the left side of the road so I'll take the westbound lanes and leave the other to you, shall we head out and do this?"

"Yeah, that breeze is cold and those ice crystals that are in it are no fun either." Leading off TD pulled out from behind the slight protection that the cut through the hill provided and was hit with a much stronger down canyon breeze. It hadn't warmed up enough yet for the winds to change direction. So for now they would have to face into the winds and feel the cold directly on any exposed skin. It would suck, but they were better off than the missing woman.

Cathy – Tuesday Morning

She awoke suddenly and found that she was shaking from the cold. It was still dark but there seemed to be some kind of change. Looking over at her fire she realized that it seemed to be completely gone. Reaching for the flashlight that she had placed next to her she turned it on and shined the light at her small fire pit. All she could see was gray ash. Thinking to herself she said, "I really, really hope that there is still something there." She shuddered as she remembered the difficulty she had when she had first started this fire. She, as cold as she was right now did not want a repeat of that. So setting the flashlight down so the light would shine on her pit she took a stick and carefully stirred up the ash and was rewarded with some small glowing coals lying deep within the ash. The further she dug the more there seemed to be. So spreading the gray ash away from these coals she carefully put some of her smaller sticks on the glowing coals and hoped that there was enough life in them to start the sticks burning. She almost held her breath, as a couple of the smaller sticks seemed to smoke a little and then blacken. But other that there just didn't seem to be enough life to get them burning. Desperate she started gently blowing on the coals and was rewarded with an increase of the glow and additional smoke coming off her sticks. She continued gently blowing and watched as some of the sticks seemed to be consumed without ever catching fire.

She turned around and looked at her great supply and tried to find the smallest sticks she could find. With this search she also looked for some additional dead grass. But knowing that most of it was still damp she thought that she would only use a little of it to mix with her wood. Not knowing how long the coals were going to last, and not wanting to have to start over, she hurried her search and this time began with a mix of the dead grass and sticks. Again she blew on the coals and briefly was rewarded with a small flame that went instantly out. Her teeth were chattering so badly now that it was difficult to blow on the coals. Almost screaming from the frustration of having the fire appear and then go out, she stopped a moment, sat still and gathered her wits, knowing again that if she lost it that she could still cause her own death. That fire meant life to her right now and it wasn't happening . . . It just wasn't happening at all. So taking a deep breath through her chattering teeth she tried again. This time keeping a good supply of small sticks and grass close by so that if she got a flame again then she would be able to nurse her small fire. How long could she depend on these coals? So once again and carefully she placed her small sticks and grasses on the coals and blew on them. In her hand she had additional sticks so that if they started to burn she would be able to add wood to her small fire.

It almost seemed like a lifetime but eventually after many failures and some close successes, she was able to finally get some of the sticks to stay burning. Slowly and carefully she continued to add the sticks to her very weak fire. It seemed that every time that she would add another stick that the fire would almost go out again. Yet eventually the fire grew in size and then eagerly began to consume the wood as she continued to feed it. Finally she knew that the fire was going to stay lit. Now adding larger pieces to the fire she could finally feel the heat starting to come from the fire. She placed her hands over the small growing fire to warm them as she continued to feed it. Slowly as she warmed her teeth quit chattering, and while still very cold she got as close as she dared to her fire. The heat now coming off of it was almost enough to cause her to want to back away. But where her body was not facing the fire she was cold, *so very cold*. So she continued to rotate to try and warm all of her. Slowly the space she was in warmed a little. She knew that with all the holes and such that it would never get hot. But any heat was welcome.

With so much effort being expended on getting her fire going again she had not realized that there had been a change in the weather. Suddenly she realized that it was quiet, *the winds were gone*. The only sounds she heard were the crackling of her small fire. Had the storm finally blown itself out? The problem for her now was that it was still dark, and by being in her shelter here she could not see anything. Listening hard for anything she heard nothing, nothing at all. It was very quiet. Then making a decision she thought that maybe it would be a good idea if she crawled out of her shelter and took a look. After all, if it were still snowing she would know immediately. So building up her fire a little she took her flashlight and crawled and worked her way back out of her protection, eventually emerging at the edge of the meadow. She caught her breath at the beauty that surrounded her. The storm was gone and now it was clear, with a full moon. The stars were so bright it was as if she could reach up and touch them. The moonlight, reflecting off the snow and trees, left it appearing to be a fairytale land or some place that existed in one of the many fantasies that had been written. It appeared to be a world untouched by man, and existing outside his influence. Captivated and awed by this beauty it was a little while before she realized that she was getting cold and was shivering again. So reluctantly she crawled back into her sanctuary to get warm and wait for daylight. How soon that would be, she really had no idea. But at least with the storm gone she felt now she would have a better chance. Not wanting her fire to go out again she remained close to it and continued to add wood. Again she marveled at how little it now took to make her comfortable. She definitely would have laughed if someone had suggested it to her before this all had happened.

Now with flickering light from her warming fire she checked her supplies once again. She thought it was a good time to turn on the handi-talkie, but as she went through the pack it wasn't there. Desperately she thought. *Where is it?* Thinking back she suddenly realized that she had left it on that rear shelf in the car. "Damn!" All she could do was shake her head. She had done it again. This was the fourth day since the accident had happened and somehow she was still alive. But now with this morning she would finish the last of her food and while water wasn't an issue, being surrounded by it as she was, food now was. As cold as it seemed to be she knew that her need for food would be greater. As it was, she had stretched out what she had, but even with that she had reached the end of her meager supply. "Well, Cath' you really have got to find your way out of this today." She admonished herself under her breath. Thinking about it by her fire she knew that she did not want to go back the way she had come, as that was where those wild animals were. And one thing for sure, she did not want to become their next meal. That meant she could only go forward or ahead and hope that eventually that these mountains would allow her to find that elusive road and safety. Thinking about it she figured that with the storm gone that she should be able to cover a greater distance. She suddenly remembered with the snow on the ground that hiking through the area would not be a simple thing with the snow hiding many small depressions and traps. She had to be careful, very careful or she could still injure herself, beside the fact it would slow her down. And if that happened it was over, plain and simple, finished. Again, not knowing the time of day or night, she hoped that it would be light soon. Right now she felt somewhat refreshed, and sore. She knew that she had slept hard last evening as she had been exhausted, and emotionally drained. She never even remembered falling asleep, and she suspected that if she hadn't gotten cold that she would have slept well into the day.

Sitting by the fire she put her backpack back together and then took the New Testament and began reading again. "Where is the wise man? Where is the scholar? Where is the philosopher of this age? Has not God made foolish the wisdom of this world? For since in the wisdom of God the world through its wisdom did not know him, God was pleased through the foolishness of what was preached to save those who believe. Jews demand miraculous signs and the Greeks look for wisdom, but we preach Christ crucified: a stumbling block to Jews and foolishness to Gentiles, but to those whom God has called, both Jews and Greeks, Christ the power of God and the wisdom of God. For the foolishness of God is wiser than man's wisdom, and the weakness of God is stronger than man's strength. 1Cor 1, 20-25." She realized when reading this passage that it was simply stating a truth about this God that she had tried to avoid. She had been seeking the wisdom of this world and ignoring the wisdom of God and his book, the Bible. Much was being revealed to her as she made this unexpected journey. Yet she had to admit that this had been here all the time just waiting patiently for her to find it. She packed the little book away and found that once again, as it is almost every morning, she needed to relieve herself. So now, with practiced ease, she went to the edge of her little sanctuary and filled her cup and then dumped it out – followed by repacking it in one of the outer compartments of the pack. At this point it seemed that things had lightened a little. So to check, she crawled back outside and when she came out she could see the grayness of dawn. Soon she would be on her way. It was still too dark to actually see any of the landscape, but it was time to make sure all was well. In a way she would be sorry to bid farewell to her small respite and sanctuary, as it had been a place that had kept her safe and somewhat warm from the fury of the storm. Once she left she probably would never be back. Heck, she suspected that once her tracks disappeared from the snow she would never be able to find it anyway.

So once back inside she let her fire burn down to coals, and then taking one last look around the now familiar shadowed area she headed out seeing the blue sky for the first time since Saturday when this all began. Looking around she felt that she could easily be the only person in this whole world. It was a very lonely feeling and she shivered, and not just from the cold. She quickly headed out keeping the hillside to her left side. Thinking as she went that this reminded her of leaving the lodge in the mornings on some of the ski trips she had taken in the past. The crispness of the air, the cloudless blue sky, all were exhilarating, with the anticipation of a great day of skiing. One thing for sure, she would never be taking such things for granted any more. As the sun rose above the trees and mountains she now was able to see this area for the first time. With the winds and the storm her visibility had only been a few feet ahead of her. Now the panorama opened all around her. The pines covered heavily in their blanket of snow, the white contrasting the green of the trees. It was like a great amount of white frosting had been placed on each of these many trees, and in areas where the land had been protected from the winds large ice sickles hung down. Sparkling in the sunlight demanding her attention over the whiteness of the snow that lay everywhere. It was almost like each one of these wonders was calling out to her saying, "Look at me! See my beauty; I am one of God's creations. If you listen quietly you can hear the song that is here." Off in the distance she could hear what sounded like a thundering. But it was too distant to be able to identify what it was. Her breath was coming out in great white clouds that would slowly disappear and the snow was crunching under her feet. As she continued to hike the thundering sound was slowly getting louder. Then ahead of her she saw the source. A large stream or small river was flowing ahead and to her right. At this point she was still trekking through that large meadow, making it easy for her to walk up to the edge of the water. Following it for a distance she stopped and caught her breath. The roaring here was very loud and carefully she went ahead and then looked over a precipice where the river dropped over the side in a huge waterfall, which was throwing up a great mist creating small rainbows. It had to be at least a couple of hundred feet straight down.

Carefully approaching the edge as close as she dared she looked out over the valley that lay below her. She could see no obvious roads or trails, and with the area heavily covered in trees, looking carefully she could see where the water disappeared into those trees, and every once in a while catch a reflection of the water among them. The beauty of what she was seeing took her breath away once again. She had no words to even describe what she was seeing. She remembered, when she was a child, that her dad had tried to explain this to her, when they went on those family outings she had hated. Now, for the first time in her life, she was seeing what he had tried to show her. This scene held her captivated for a while, then coming back to reality she knew that she had to move on. Looking as far as she could into the valley and the surrounding areas she firstly could see no way down from here, and secondly, nothing to give promise of rescue. So backing away from her perch she headed back to the meadow's edge again placing the hillside to her left side to continue her hike – hopefully to safety. There, by the running water, she refilled a couple of her water bottles just to make sure she would have enough water. She had to be very careful, as the surface near the edge of the rapidly running water had a film of ice, making the surface extremely slippery. The last thing she needed right now was to fall into that water. Especially since she had no way to dry off or get warm or even have anything to change into. While water seemed to be everywhere she couldn't count on it always being that way. Both the hillside and the meadow now turned away from the stream and the cliff and as earlier, the day before, turned out to be a finger that she worked around. Not one to really know anything about direction other than left and right she thought now, with the change in direction that she had just made that finally she might actually be heading in the right direction. Slowly the meadow narrowed and she found that the trees on the right were now closing in and the hillside on her left was dropping down a little. Just ahead of her she saw what looked like a trail. The first one she could remember seeing. Of course she might have been on one but with the storm and the amount of snow on the ground she would never had known.

When she reached the trail she found a park service sign there. Brushing off the snow she read what it said. "IN THIS MEADOW IN THE EARLY 1800'S A GROUP OF TRAPPERS MADE A STAND AGAINST A WARRING BAND OF

INDIANS. OF THE GROUP OF TWENTY MEN ONLY TWO SURVIVED THE ATTACK, AND WAS FINALLY ABLE TO ESCAPE." *Wow!* Was all she could say. Others had been here and some had actually died. At least she knew that she had found a maintained trail. But knowing nothing about it she had no idea how long it was, where it started, or even if this was the end point. But it was better than nothing – which is exactly what she had up until now. She was finding that even with her exercise, she was having difficulty in keeping warm. It had to be very cold. Even when the sun finally had made its appearance it had not warmed things up. While emotionally it was cheering to see the blue skies and sunlight, the weak sun seemed to have no heat at all. She knew that this was an illusion, and the cold air was from the storm that had just left the area. Now looking at the trail, which showed as a lower point in the snow, she realized that immediately she would be back under trees and shadow, where it probably would be colder still. Yet what could she do? For the first time since leaving her wrecked car she had found a possible way out of her dilemma. Unsure and hesitating for only a moment she shrugged and headed down the trail. After all what choice did she have?

Immediately she was bathed in shadows and definitely could feel an increase in the cold air. She shivered as it hit her. Now what? The hiking she was presently doing wasn't warming her at all, and it had during the storm. While not freezing she thought she couldn't be far from it. Again her breath came out in great white clouds only to dissipate quickly. She picked up her pace to both move along and get more of her blood circulating, hoping that the faster movement would increase her internal warmth. Since she was now on a trail, even one that was covered with snow, she thought, most likely, there would be little chance of tripping over something or falling into a ditch or hole. Right now it seemed that more of the danger lies in the cold than in the trail. She followed the snow covered trail as it curved around the hillside keeping somewhat flat. That curve she felt was taking her away from the highway again, but who knew for sure, she surely didn't. Then the trail broke out of the trees into another meadow – this one being smaller than the one she had just left. But now where did the trail leave this one? At least there was one consolation in coming back out into a meadow. It meant that once again she was in the full sun, and when she had left the shadows she could sense more than feel a difference in the temperature. Looking around before hiking on, she said, "Okay Cath' where does this trail leave the meadow?" With no answer she looked across the meadow and seemed to see what appeared to be a depression running across the meadow off to her right. Thinking about it she realized that back when she had camped with the family, as a child, when they would walk the trails around the campsite that the trails seemed to be a little lower than the surrounding ground. "Okay then, at this point I've nothing to lose and much to gain so why not." She knew that she just couldn't stand there. She was out of food and running out of time. It was "do it now", for sure, either she move or just quit and die. This made her think of the New Testament and the 40 days that Christ spent in the desert. Shaking her head she said, "Now what I would give right now for some of that heat." Yet she now had a better appreciation of what it may have been like. Christ had to survive the harsh conditions and at the same time face temptations when he could be at his weakest. Her time lost in this wilderness was not even close to Christ's trials, but every inch had been a struggle to survive, and she wasn't close to being out of the danger as of yet. Would she have given in to those temptations that the Devil presented? For that question she had no answer, so she headed off across the meadow.

Looking up she saw that the sun had climbed higher in the sky, but again it felt no warmer. If she wasn't in such a desperate situation, she might have been able to stop and enjoy this beauty that surrounded her. Yet, because the time seemed to be flying by, she needed to move. Once the day ended she would need to find shelter. She suddenly realized that she was hungry, but had nothing to eat.

Everything was gone and she suspected that her body was burning the calories faster trying just to keep warm. Reaching the opposite side of the meadow she saw no obvious trail. Then working her way up and down this opposite side from where she had entered the meadow, she finally found that the trail. Once across the meadow, the trail had taken a sharp left and coming from the direction she had just come from, this change of direction was not visible or expected. But there before her was a trail marker to confirm that she was now where she needed to be. Once again she would have to go under the trees into the shadows and into colder air. Off to her left a ravine lay below the trail and to her right ran an up-slope. The trail wound and twisted through the trees and the hills until finally she had no idea what direction she really was going. She found as she dropped down into lower areas that the air would be very cold, only to slowly warm slightly when she would climb out of these low areas. As far a she knew, because of the twisting of the trail, she could find herself right back in the same meadows, and because she would arrive from a different direction would not recognize it as a place she had been. Now both her feet and hands were numb, and even though she had her ears covered they seemed to be very cold. She was *losing* the battle against this cold. Her breathing was ragged from the exertion she was putting forth, and her lungs burned both from the cold air and from the exercise. She knew that shortly she would have to take a break, but wanted it to be somewhere in the sunlight and not under the trees. Again she had to admit she was very scared. She had thought that once the storm broke and the sun came out that it would be easier. Yes the hiking had been easier, but she hadn't factored in the temperature, which had grown dangerously cold because of those clear skies. Panic lurked below the surface. If she lost it now could she get herself back under control?

Late Tuesday Afternoon – Hillstown Search and Rescue

After taking a lunch break TD and Jacob continued their searches with Jacob now working the north areas off the road and TD the south areas. All the checks from the other teams had produced nothing. In the obvious locations other than what was still there, they had come up empty. There wasn't much light left but at least most of their area had been searched. He suspected that it was much the same for Bob and Reggie. So far Paul and Art had come up empty also. He was becoming a little discouraged from the lack of success. He had felt so sure that they would find something by now. Well, at least they were working back towards their starting point, and then once there, they would head back to the meeting point. *What if nothing is found?* Would this be another one of those accidents that would not be discovered until spring? He didn't believe it to be so, as he had such a strong feeling that just would not go away, about this one. Of course as strong as this last storm had been the wreck could easily be covered in snow and they could just pass by with none the wiser.

* * *

Paul and Art had the smallest area to search but that simply was because theirs was the furthest out, leaving them less time to search and to find anything. So far there had been no signs of any accident in the areas where any of them had searched. No damaged railings no bruised trees, no broken anything to indicate something happened here. The two were presently beyond the bridge, which covered the rapidly flowing stream that never seemed to freeze over no matter how cold it got. Just ahead of them was an area, because of shadow and curves, a place where many TC's had happened in the past. After the bridge the road climbed a bit and while it did this it went into an "S" curve. Again because of the shadow many times this curve would not be recognized for what it was until it was too late. Then people would enter into it much too fast running off the road. The second problem with it lay with that same shadow. It seemed to be one of the first areas to develop black ice, giving it the local name of "little dead man's curve". Yet on close inspection there seemed to be no new wounds to any of the large trees that bordered the road at this point. Climbing up the hill they peaked out at the top, and looking carefully, saw nothing.

They reached the end of their search area, broke for lunch and then after checking in Paul headed off the road on the north side and Art took the south. Here, in this area, it would be a difficult trek as there was few pathways and heavy cover of timber and vegetation. The berry bushes especially were nasty with them covering acres of land. Where the snow had covered them it was an illusion that the area would be easy to work. When one attempted to go over the top of them you had just as much chance of falling through into the patches as staying on top. The thorns on these bushes were vicious. So trying to stay close to the road, at times, was near impossible. There were a number of times where they would have to stop the snowmobile, get off and work their way on foot back towards the road to get close enough to inspect it. It was slow and hard work, with no success for any of the teams so far. Where did this car leave the road? This was now the conclusion, since the road had been completely searched through all their respective areas. Of course it could have happened beyond their search areas, but it was hoped that the accident, if there had been one, would be within the selected areas. Surprisingly, to Paul, it took them a long time to work their way back to that stream. Once there, Paul knew that they would have to backtrack a little, as there was no way to cross this stream. And looking at the embankment that led up to the road he knew that neither he himself or the machine could climb up there because of the steep angle and the materials used to build this portion of the road. Calling TD on the radio he said, "TD, I'm on the east side of that stream. There has been nothing found east of here, and if she crashed to the west of here she wouldn't be able to cross this stream on foot. Plus, from what I can see, there is no easy . . . no . . . there is no way to the road here. If someone went off the road on the other side, further up and out of our search area, this would be a block, and if they went off to the west they would be forced that way back towards you guys . . . by the way, not that you don't know this, but it's bitter cold out here. I for one wouldn't want to be out in this without the proper gear. It's almost worse than the storm."

"Okay, Paul. Light is against us here, and we are almost out of time. You're going to have to backtrack, right?"

"Yeah, there's just no way up, and it'll cost us time we don't have, but there's little choice."

"Okay, do the best you can. So far everyone has come up empty, and we have almost finished our area here. Still that sun is setting and light is becoming a factor already."

"Okay then, see you all back at the meeting area. Unless we find something that will be the next contact I'll make with you." As Paul concluded his conversation, waiting for a response from TD he shook his head. *Just where is the accident, the TC?* He had been hopeful that by now there would have been some word, but nothing, just nothing.

"Okay then, see you back at the meeting point." Shaking his head TD thought. *Who'd of thought that something like a car could be so hard to find?* Gunning the snowmobile and then moving out, he continued working his area.

It took Paul a little while backtracking to find a place he could get back on the road and then past the stream. It left him and Art very little light left to finish their area, and they still had to find a way back down the embankment to continue working the areas they needed to search. With both of them meeting at the bridge they conversed briefly and then headed west on the road to find an access to the lower area. They were both going slow studying the roadside to find a way down. As they continued searching both suddenly stopped and looked at each other with Paul asking, "Did you catch that?" Then looking at Art he continued, "I guess you did since you stopped as quickly as I did." Dismounting, they slowly backtracked and again caught a flash of light reflecting off of something. Carefully moving just beyond the bright area, so as not to be blinded, they both looked closer. "Hey Paul", Art asked, "Doesn't that look like glass there?" Both moved closer to the shoulder of the road and searched hard for the source.

Finally locating what appeared to be a small area among the snow that was glass. "You know", Paul commented, "That could just be a piece of broken glass or even something from an earlier wreck that wasn't cleaned up."

"True, but we can't tell from up here. How in the heck are we going to get down there?"

"Well", Paul said, "Before we do that let's look closer at the surrounding area and see if we can see any sign that something happened here." They then began to walk carefully up and down the road studying the surrounding countryside for anything that could help them identify this as the right place. Paul, studying the railing placed there to keep cars on the road, finally found a slight mark that could have been new. While he was doing this Art studied the edge of the road and the trees to see if he could find anything. Walking back to the west he stopped and turned back to the east and then excitedly yelled at Paul. ""Paul come here! Look at this!"

Getting up from his kneeling position Paul went back to join Art. When he got there his asked, "Okay what have you found that gotten you so excited?" Art pointed at one of the many groves of trees that sat right at the road edge and said as he pointed, "Paul if you look carefully you can see what appear to be broken branches in a number of those trees, and then that one there has a large scar. It's easy to miss and if you aren't at the right angle it's completely invisible.

At first I thought it was an illusion, but by moving a little I could see it plainly."

Trying to follow where Art was pointing he moved around and looked hard, "Sorry I still don't see it." Then moving again to change his angle he then said, "Okay . . . I think . . . yes I do think I see what you are looking at. And yes, you are right. It's very easy to miss. But you wonder how, as that is a good-sized mark. And now looking I think I can see the broken branches that create a path right to that scar. Good job. Now we've got to figure out how we can get down there to confirm that it's what we are looking for. Tell you what, take your snowmobile further up and see if you can find a way down. I'll walk it for a little distance and if one of us finds a way we'll call each other on the radio. Oh I do hope this is it. But until we get down there and check it out I don't want to call TD. Let's get to it."

It took them thirty minutes before they could find a way down off the road. Between the heavy growths of trees and the angle of the slope from the road they had to backtrack quite a distance to find a way down that was somewhat safe. As it was they had to go the whole distance on foot. It required fighting through the trees and brush that seemed to almost close the whole area off. Then they ran into the wild berry bushes and their heavy thorns. Finally pushing through with many scratches and gouges they came into an open pathway that they were able to follow back in the direction of their possible discovery to be able to investigate what they had seen from the road. Art, turning towards Paul said. "You know Paul; we need to find a better way back up to the road. It was hard, well near impossible, getting down here the way we did. But I think it will be doubly tough to go back that way. I believe that the only way we would find where we entered this path is by our tracks in the snow. Without them we would easily walk right by. Look, even with these heavy clothes I am wearing I must be bleeding from at least a half of dozen places from those thorns."

"Yeah that was no picnic for sure. Now, after we have worked so hard to get here, let's hope that our effort doesn't turn into a wild goose chase." He paused a moment before continuing. "Plus this is the last chance for us today. We are going to barely beat the setting sun." It took an additional fifteen minutes for them to get to the site, and there before them sat the car. On the downhill side the color and side of the car was plainly visible. "Art clear some of that snow from the back and see if you can uncover the license plate so that we can confirm. I hate to inform them we found it and find out it was one that was just similar. It would be embarrassing as well as getting their hopes up only to disappoint. While you do that I'm going to see if I can open any of the doors. Be careful this doesn't look to be in the safest of positions. It really looks like this thing could continue down the hill at any moment."

Art, nodding in agreement, went to the back and carefully dug away the snow, and then grabbed Paul's attention as he pointed at the rear window. "Look at that, there probably isn't much more than a couple of square inches visible of that window. If we hadn't been where we were when we were, we would never have caught that reflection from the sun." He continued to dig down through the snow and finally uncovered the plates. With numb hands he carefully dug out a piece of paper from one of his pockets, which had the license number on it and compared it. "This is the car the license matches."

"Okay I guess now comes the moment of truth." Paul said. "Let's see if we have a body. But before I do that I think I'll call TD and let him know that we found the car and that we are investigating it presently. That way they can call off any additional searching." Pulling the radio off his belt he called and said, "TD this is Paul." He waited for a response not knowing if his signal could get out from down in this area. With no immediate response he repeated his attempt and waited again. Eventually he was rewarded with a weak response from TD. "Yes Paul, this is TD, but your signal is weak. I can barely make you out – had to shut down the machine. What do you have for us?"

"The good news is that we have found the TC. Right now we just confirmed the license plate so that we weren't passing on some bad information. We are still investigating and are just about to try and get inside the car. Let's say it was luck that allowed us to find it. The car is completely buried on the uphill side with snow and completely hidden."

"Sounds great, where is it?"

"Oh, sorry about that. You know the bridge that covers that rapidly flowing stream, the bridge that's just before 'little dead mans', it left the road on the west side of that bridge. Traveling almost all the way down and then ended up being wedged against some of the trees. It sits on the north side of the road. Once we finish the inspection I'll contact you again. We are running out of light. So with this inspection I think we will be done for the night. Contact in the next few."

"Okay then, we'll be waiting." TD replied. He followed up by making contact with Bob. "Bob did you catch that?"

"Yeah, it was weak here also but I caught it. You know that would have been the last place I would have looked. There normally isn't an issue there. It's usually in those curves."

Paul turned towards Art and warning him. "Okay Art, let's be very careful here. You stand down at the bottom and away from the car while I inspect the inside. That way if it begins to slide you will be out of the way and then if I need help you will be there."

"Okay boss, works for me." Art carefully worked his way back down to the bottom and backed away. Paul, once he could see that Art was away, looked closely and saw that the front door was pinned by one of the trees leaving the back door as the only one that he would be able to open. Looking carefully, it appeared that the snow by this door was somewhat packed, as if someone had exited and entered here a number of times. Surprisingly the door opened easily, the last thing he expected. It was somewhat dark inside because of the time of day and it being buried in the snow so he reached in his belt pouch and took out a flashlight. Then steeling himself he ran the light up front to the driver's seat. Two things hit him immediately. The first was no body, actually no one at all. The second was that the seats had been cannibalized for their covers. Then yelling out to Art he said, "No one home, and I would guess she was alive for quite a while waiting out the storm. I'm going to continue to look here in a minute, but I need to get out and contact TD again."

"That's good news, I think." Art said, "But if she isn't there where is she?"

"Very good question. While I am bringing TD up to date and searching the car why not look around the area. She may be close by. We surely aren't out of the woods on this one yet. Plus we really are out of time. Make it a quick one." Taking the time, being really careful, and taking the radio off his belt he contacted

TD and let him know that the woman wasn't in her car. So at least they knew she had been alive after the crash. He gingerly climbed back into the car and with the flashlight searched for anything to help them. There was trash lying around showing that she had food and had been here a number of days. *Okay then, where is she now?* Then looking on top of the dash he saw a piece of paper and under it an envelope. Reaching carefully for them he hit the pieces slightly and they slid off the dash onto the floor down by the brake pedal. Shaking his head he said to himself, "Why does it seem that when things drop like this that they end up going to the furthest and most difficult area?" Of course he had no answer. So with care and struggling a little he was finally able to recover the two items. At this point breathing a little hard from the exertion and effort of recovering the papers he got out of the car and closed the door. The first thing he saw was what appeared to be a sealed envelope addressed to her family, the other simply said, "I'm alive and it's Monday. I am leaving my car and heading back to find help. Plan on finding a way back to the road and following it back the way I came." And here it was Tuesday early evening, which meant she had been gone from her car for at least 36 hours. Included in that time period was the fury of the storm as it blew itself out. They had been up the length of the road well past the wreck site, and while they hadn't been specifically looking for anyone, if she had made it to the road then there should have been something. At a loss as to what to do he contacted TD and brought him up to date. Darkness was falling rapidly they needed to leave. "Art, Art where are you?" Paul yelled.

"Over here Paul, in this copse of trees. I found a place that she used for her nature calls. She definitely was alive. What did you find out?"

"Tell you as we leave. We are out of time and we have to find a way back to the road and the snowmobiles and then head in. I think tomorrow will be very interesting for all of us." As they worked their way back out attempting to find another point in which to return to the road, the dusk light didn't help. Even though the place that they had chosen turned out to be somewhat easier, it was no picnic. They found that they were not very close to their equipment when they finally emerged back on the road, leaving them no choice but to backtrack to where they had parked their snowmobiles. As the hiked back to their snowmobiles Paul filled Art in about the note he had found in the car. They climbed back on the snowmobiles, letting TD know that they were on their way. TD responded saying that the rest would start the trek back into town, but travel slowly, so as to give him and Art time to get closer. They all would meet at the firehouse, and then go in for a meal at the café. At least in the light of another day they would have a starting point to search for the missing person.

But there would be nothing to track because of the storm – the only clue being that cryptic note. It was going to be like searching for the infamous needle in the haystack.

* * *

It was dark when they finally arrived back at the firehouse. Seeing the other snowmobiles parked there, Paul and Art went inside. There they were greeted by the other members of the search team, all with questioning looks upon their faces. "Okay guys I can see that you are all curious." Then looking directly at TD Paul said. "TD here's the note and envelope we found in the wreck. My guess would be that she hit some black ice and spun off the road. If you remember, we had just had that partial thaw then this last storm arrived, which I suspect probably created that ice. Anyway the car went airborne breaking some branches followed by contacting one of the trees directly. I believe it fell down to where it ended up between a number of trees where it became wedged. Still, looking at the wreck, it could have, at any time, continued its slide down the hillside. With the amount of new snow we had, the upper side was completely buried in snow and invisible. Even without the snow where the car ended up would have made it almost impossible to see from the road. There was a lot of damage to the car, but she was lucky that all the windows stayed in place. While both the windshield and the driver door window were damaged they stayed put. From what we could determine she, from her statement in the note, stayed with the car until Monday morning. I think that she felt that there would be no one to come and help her, so she would have to help herself. She now has been away from her car for close to 36 hours. Not a good thing really, as this means she would have been outside of her car when the final fury of that storm hit. It was almost worse than most of the storm. Of course it makes our job much more difficult since the storm would have wiped out anything that would have been marked by her passing. Where the TC happened there was absolutely no easy way to get back to the road. We had to fight our way through in both directions. So I feel that she probably went the way of least resistance thinking that a little ways down it would be a simple thing to return to the road. Now that we have been up and down that road a number of times I can pretty much assume that she never made it back to the road . . . So now what?"

"Good question Paul", TD responded, "At this moment I don't honestly know. This surely complicates things. Bob what is your thought on this? Actually let's wait. I've talked with Faith and she is waiting down at the café to feed us. Let's head there and continue our discussion." They all agreed and headed out to the snowmobiles and drove over to the café for an evening meal.

* * *

Later, after everything broke up, with them planning to continue the search on Wednesday at daylight, TD returned home, tired from the day of searching. Sighing and shaking his head when Laura asked if they had been successful in finding the missing woman he said. "At least we were partly successful."

With an inquisitive look she asked. "Partially successful, what do you mean by that? How can you be partially successful?"

Smiling a sad smile and staring off into the distance he said. "Her wrecked car was located, but she wasn't with it. I haven't actually been on the site of the TC yet . . ."

Interrupting Laura said, "You haven't been there yet, what are you doing here? I mean if she was ours I would expect you to be out there doing something, anything to get this taken care of."

Throwing his hands up in surrender he continued. "I know, I know, but the car wasn't found until almost dark. Plus it was in a place that was almost impossible to get to. It was Paul and Art that finally found it and even with their experience it took them quite a while to find a way to the wreck. But, there was no body and no one around at all."

"Are you sure it's the right one and not another one that might not have been reported?"

"Now you know me better than that. When they finally were able to get to the wreck they confirmed the license plate. Plus inside the wreck she had left a note saying that she was leaving and would be trying to rescue herself."

"And you mean you didn't go after her when this was found?"

"Wait a minute Laura, at this juncture there is nothing we can do."

"Nothing you can do? You possibly still have someone out there without any practical experience that may still be alive and you're telling me there's nothing that can be done? This doesn't sound like you Terry."

Shaking his head and again throwing his hands in the air he said, "Okay Laura what would you do? Here's what we are facing. She left the car on Monday. You remember what Monday was like right?" She nodded agreement and he continued. "There is nothing, no trail, no direction, and it was dark by the time Art and Paul got back on the road. Other than the note she left we have nothing to work with. We simply ran out of time. Tomorrow we will be all searching very hard. But now, with what we know, I don't hold out much hope for her rescue. Yeah I know I have felt strongly that she was alive, and that has proven to have been correct, but to have no experience, and to been out in what that storm unleashed yesterday, I just don't see how she could have survived that." Taking a deep breath he let it out slowly saying, Laura I need a shower, and then we can sit down and continue, but to tell the truth here, it has been a hard day and I am beat."

"Oh I'm sorry. I kind of just ambushed you at the door and didn't even let you really even get inside. Okay, go take your shower. I'll put on some fresh coffee, unless your coffee'd out."

"No some fresh coffee would be great. The shower should give me a chance to think on this problem some more." He said his greetings to his three children who were in different rooms, filled them in on what he knew, and went to take his shower.

Laura, as she went into the kitchen to get the coffee started, realized that he had said something about a note. She thought, for a moment, to go and bother him about it, but thought better about it and decided to wait until he came back out. She needed to make sure that the children had wrapped up their homework and chores anyway. This "mother stuff" was never done anyway – not that Terry didn't help, because he did. Still it seemed that more fell on her shoulders than his. "Oh well, it seems to have always been that way." She said quietly as she shrugged. After checking in on the children she went to the dining room and sat at the table awaiting Terry to return from his shower. With her head on her thumbs as she thought about this Terry came into the room. "Ah, I think I can see that you've got something on your mind. You always do that when you are thinking or have something that's very important to you that you have just thought about."

"Do I? You know I didn't even realize that I do that. Can I get you some coffee now?"

Shaking his head he said, "No, no that's all right. You're sitting and I'm still standing. So I think I can find the kitchen."

"Are you sure? I mean it seems like the last place I would find a man." She laughed, knowing that Terry helped her in the kitchen. But she had friends that complained about their husbands all the time, and how they just didn't help them at all. She was thankful to be in the type of relationship that she had. A very thoughtful and considerate man who helped whenever he could, and would drop anything he was doing to give her assistance. At times she thought she would like to join the other women in men bashing, but just couldn't.

Smiling and looking at her he asked, "Let's see here, hmmm . . ." Then glancing up and putting his hand up to his chin he continued " . . . let's see, if I remember right that's where the food is. And if that's where the food is I think I'll have no problem locating it if only by the smell alone."

Smiling she said, "Are you sure? I mean we women are known to have much better sniffers than you men."

Then getting a look of devilment in his eyes and then smiling, he said, "Ah yes and I think I know why. It helps when I want to get real close to you."

Laughing she then said. "Now let's not go there. After all we are in mixed company here. Besides I have something else I need to talk about. We can talk about the other after we go to bed tonight."

Still with mischief in his eyes he responded, "Are you sure?" Then on a more serious note he continued. "I just love to tease you. Yeah I'll go get my coffee and come back. Then you can hit me with what you want to ask. Remember you're the one who started it."

"Started what?"

"The teasing of course."

"Did not."

"Did too."

As they continued on this vein the oldest daughter came into the dining room and said, "Mom! Dad! Would you two just quit! You two sound like my brothers when they argue."

They then looked at each and laughed. Laura, turning to her daughter said, "Sorry about that we didn't realize that we were that loud. I know this is a small house, but we didn't really think anyone was listening."

Sarah continued on into the kitchen. There they could hear a cupboard open, followed by the refrigerator as she poured herself a glass of milk.

"Mom, could I grab a couple of cookies before my brothers devour them?"

Nodding and understanding completely, Laura said, "Yes, a couple would be fine. Just bring the dishes back when you are finished."

"Yes, mother . . . and thanks." At which point she headed back through the dining room and returned to her room.

"Would you like a couple before, as she said, the boys clean us out?"

"I'll get them since I haven't quite sat down yet. I am assuming that you want a couple also. What do you want to drink with them? I'll have my coffee." Terry said as he headed into the kitchen.

Thinking a minute still with her head resting on her hands she said, "I think coffee will be fine for me also."

A short time later Terry brought in a plate of cookies and returned to get the two cups of coffee, which he brought back, placed one in front of her and went around the table and sat across from her. Putting his cup on the table and with both arms placed on the table leaned forward and said, "Okay my dear one; I know when something is really bothering you so please go ahead."

Looking across into his eyes Laura asked. "If I remember it right, you said that a note was found in the car? So are you going to call the families to let them know what you have found?"

Pausing a moment before answering he said. "No, I don't think so. I've thought about it after the wreck was located, and after when Paul searched it and found the note, but she was long gone. So there's very little to really pass on. Plus, until I have something really concrete to be able to tell them either good or bad, I don't want to get their hopes up just to have them dashed."

"Wait a minute here. Are you telling me you're not going to give them anything at all?"

"Yeah . . . It's always a difficult decision, but one that has to be made. You know, when do you finally inform the families? In this case I want to wait."

Thinking a little before she answered Laura said. "Okay. Now I am a mother of our three children. If any one of them were in this same situation I guarantee that I would want to know everything at the very moment something new was found. Our daughter just came through here. If it had been her you can believe that firstly, I would be a wreck, but secondly I would want to have information . . . any information good or bad. Not knowing would be hell. Then, if I found out later that something was known, but it wasn't given to me I would be angry. I know in the end it is your decision. But I am your wife, and I think I have a right to put in my two cents about this and of course other things."

Smiling he said. "And you do it so well too. Yes it is always a hard decision, and, believe me, I always welcome your comments. We are partners for life, and I take what you say seriously." Then smiling once again he continued. "I'd better or else. I can understand perfectly why it is important to know. But at this moment I feel that I would be raising hopes where I shouldn't. I really have nothing, nothing at all that would make any difference. So I think that until we either find something tomorrow, or not find anything by tomorrow night, I am going to hold off. I promise you that if by tomorrow night if she isn't found then I will call the families and let them know everything that I have."

Looking at him with some consternation in her eyes she asked. "What did you mean by that statement?"

"Which one are you referring to?"

"Oh the one where you said, quote 'I'd better or else', you know that one."

Laughing he said. "Now Laura you know that women are the family center. And I've heard it said by the ones in the know that if momma isn't happy nobody is happy. And I have found it to be the truth. When you are unhappy about something either the children or I have done that wasn't what you expected or had thought was wrong . . . Well, the rest of the family has to walk on broken glass until we can make it right in your eyes. Then and only then can we breathe a sigh of relief and move on."

"I'm not that bad am I?"

Again smiling from getting a rise out her he said, "Yes you can be. You know like a momma bear protecting her cub. But that's getting off the subject. I have no need or desire to change what we have. After all from the first time we met I knew that there could be no other in my life but you. Of course we've added to the family over the years . . ."

Somewhat mollified she said, "I'm glad to hear that." Then shaking her head she returned to the original subject. "Are you sure, by tomorrow night, you will contact them one way or the other? I have your promise on that?" Then putting a stern look she usually saved for the kids she said. "And if you don't young man you will have me to answer to." Then laughing she said. "I can't say *wait until your dad gets home.*" This brought laughter from both of them, breaking the tension that had been building briefly.

"Laura you have my promise. I have no desire to hold anything from the loved ones of a missing person. But it is always very difficult to know when it is the right time. I've done it at the wrong times in the past and have learned. So now I am more cautious before I make any comments, or family contact. It's tough no matter when you do it . . . especially if it involves death. And unfortunately this is beginning to look like one of those kinds of contact. I'm still holding out hope for a safe and happy resolution to this, but it is a very small hope at this time."

Both of them were quiet for a while. Terry sipping his coffee then commented, "Darn we were concentrating so much on our conversation that this has gotten cold. Check yours, if it's cold also I'll go microwave them and heat them up." She found that hers was cold also and handed him the cup of coffee, he went into the kitchen. She could hear the microwave open, close, and then heard the beeps associated with the timer and followed by hearing it run. In a short time Terry made his appearance with the now hot coffee, and then instead of sitting across from her sat down next to her. He set the cups down, then put his arm around her shoulders and said. "I really understand completely. You are a woman, a wife, and a mother and . . . of course also a daughter to your parents. I think until one becomes any one of these things that there is no way to fully understand what it's like.

"The toughest job you and I have is raising our children. You know that one of the book types I like to read is westerns. I guess to use an analogy from that era it would be that raising children is like taming a wild horse. They always have a mind of their own, and their direction is not necessarily the right direction, and it is up to us to correct that. But with loving discipline, and I think we've done a pretty good job so far, we can continue direct their paths in the proper direction. I just never realized before we entered into this world of parenthood just how difficult and rewarding it is. I wouldn't trade it for anything. I know that it makes it much more difficult for you and I, and at times I look back nostalgically to those times when it was just you and me. You know, leaving us free to do what we want, to be more spontaneous, something that is almost impossible now. It's like we have to literally plan everything including our intimacy. Which, by the way, I have no complaints about, it's just that it was nice when we had spontaneity, and spur of the moment stuff. Now the spur of the moment stuff has more to do with those emergency trips to the doctor because our kids did something stupid and hurt themselves. No I'm not complaining, even if it seems so. It's just, for you and me, and I'm sure for any other married couple out there, life continues to get more complicated, and it seems that there ends up being less time for the *you and me* that began those so many years ago."

Smiling a sad smile Laura said. "Yeah, that's very true." Staring off into the distance and really seeing nothing she continued. "Those were nice times weren't they? Like you I wouldn't trade a minute of what we have, nor the road that got us here. We've had some very difficult times, and at times I wonder how we got here and where have the years gone. I mean it seems like yesterday when our oldest was just born. And there we were wondering what to do. After all they didn't come with any instructions and there before us was a new life that depended completely on us. I must admit at that moment, even though my love for this new life overflowed, I felt completely inadequate. She was beautiful then, and she is now . . ." Now with a dreamy far off look in her eyes she continued in a softer tone. "It is sad how fast these years have flown by us. Soon all we will have is memories, and the children visiting us with their families. Then we truly will wonder, how did we get here at this very moment in time, and what happened to the years."

Listening he said nothing, as there was nothing to say. He agreed with her totally. Looking up at the clock he noticed it was getting late. He and Laura needed to make sure the kids were in bed and then they needed to head that way themselves. He and the search team needed to be out at the wreck site as soon as they could see. So he would be leaving the house around 4:00 am. "Laura, I hate to break this up, but look at the time. I'll put this stuff in the sink, you go say good night to the kids, and I'll do the same giving them the fatherly push towards going to sleep, and then join you in the bedroom. Oh by the way, not that you need to be reminded of it, but I am always going back before our beginnings and I remembered that I prayed to God for him to bring me the one who he had chosen for me. And I think you had done much the same thing. I know that God answers prayers in his own way, but in this one I couldn't be happier. You have been all that I could have wished for and more. I know at times because of what I do that it might seem that I don't care or don't think about you. Understand this, I always do, and always will and if it isn't obvious I very much love you."

A little embarrassed by Terry's comments she was silent for a moment and said. "Well thank you sir." Then silent again as she got up out of her chair she continued. "Now that's something for me that's kind of hard to follow. As we have talked about many times over the years, yes I prayed for you even though I had no idea who you were. Yes, there have been times over the years where I've been frustrated with you. But every time that happens I listen to some other woman complain about her relationship and her husband and know that I have no room to complain. Now I'm going to get out of here before I start crying or find that I'm embarrassing myself further." She leaned over and lightly kissed him on his cheek and then said. "Guess we will meet again shortly in the bedroom after we finish our responsibilities here. You know it really sucks having to be an adult."

Cathy – Tuesday Afternoon – Evening

As she continued down the trail, she looked around and so far there had been no place that she could see where it left the trees and placed her even briefly back into the sunlight. She so desperately wanted to take a break somewhere in the sunlight. *The shadowed areas are so cold.* Finally giving up she stopped and leaned against one of the trees that was close to the trail. As the weariness fogged her mind she only knew one thing, she had to continue to push and not give up, and it was becoming tougher by the minute just to do that. Having to pee again she began to envy her brother who only had to expose a little part to relieve himself. She, on the other hand, had to uncover her complete bottom and so far had found no other way to be able to do this. While she used to laugh at the movies where they showed those long johns with the trap door bottoms she now could appreciate and wish she had them – if they even existed anymore.

Finally both because of the cold and the need to carry on she got the strength to head out once more. A few times, during the day, she thought that far in the distance she had heard a motor running. As to what it really was, she had no idea, let alone where it was coming from. The sound had been so distant and soft that she had barely recognized it. Then once having done so, could only state that it must have been a car, but that was all. So all she could do was put one foot in front of the other and continue. The trail she was on took a sharp right and began to head up a steep hill. Stopping a moment and looking at it she didn't know if she had the strength to hike it or just stand there and give up. Then sighing and shrugging, she started the climb. It would have been tough if she hadn't been exhausted. But now it was almost impossible for her to make the climb. Forcing her way up she found that for the first time today she was warming up. In fact as she neared what she thought might be the top she found herself sweating. Well at least she wasn't cold.

Here the trail made a sharp left was level for a while and then started climbing once again. "No, no please no . . . I just don't have it." She pleaded. Staring at it dumbly, and slumped over from the fatigue that drove down through her complete being she finally got the strength from somewhere to continue. She, in her entire life, had never been this tired or ached so deeply. She knew now that unless something changed quickly that she was losing, and would at some point reach the end of what little strength she had left, and at that point it would be finished. As she climbed this new portion of the trail she found that it only went a short distance up as it curved to the left in a gentle curve and then suddenly started back down hill again on the other side. "Thank God!" she whispered as she pushed forward. Yet she was finding that even hiking downhill now required effort. And while she was now using different muscles than the ones necessary to climb it didn't matter. She was shaky and her legs were beginning to feel rubbery. *Trouble!* She worried that it would now be only a matter of time before she began to cramp. She also found that by going down hill she was no longer using the energy she used while climbing. She could feel herself cooling down, and as she got near the bottom she was becoming cold again. *How much further can it be?*

At this point she had seen nothing to indicate that she was close to civilization at all. As far as she knew she might have actually been going in the wrong direction – going deeper into the wilderness instead of heading out. When this realization hit her it brought her to a complete stop. *Now what?* Did she turn around and head back and see if she could find where the trail left that first area where she had first found it? As she thought about it she knew that there was no way that she had the energy, let alone strength, to backtrack and start over. So that only left going in the direction she was presently heading and hope that she was right. Once the decision was made she slowly began her hike again. She was very scared and very lost when the 23rd Psalm entered unbidden into her mind once again. "Yea, though I walk through the valley of death . . ." She thought that if any scripture was appropriate that this probably was right now. She knew that if things did not change very soon that she was done, finished, it would be over. She wondered, as her mind drifted, how others had felt as they neared their own death. Did they accept it or did they fight until there was nothing left to fight with? Well, she wasn't just going to give in to it. She would fight it with all that she had left. Although she had to admit that it would be nice just to lie down and rest. Letting whatever happen, happen. She found herself shivering again, and her teeth chattering. She had everything that she had brought with her on – including the material from the car seats and the emergency blanket from the backpack. It just wasn't enough.

One of the many problems she was facing was being able to see any distance ahead of her. There were so many trees that the only place that gave her any idea of where the trail led was at the points where it went straight. Now she could see that the sun was beginning to set, as every once in a while, she could see the sunlight slanting through the trees. That meant that shortly it would be getting dark, and *colder*. She still had the flashlight so the darkness shouldn't be too much of an issue. But she didn't know if she could handle any additional cold. She was barely hanging on now. And even though it seemed that the sun had thrown little heat she knew better. Once it set for the night the temperatures were going to plummet tremendously. She had to find shelter, and find it quickly. But so far there had been nothing – no place which would provide any protection like that other place she had spent the night. Here it was just the trail, and the trees.

It suddenly became dark as the sun dropped behind the mountains. She stopped and dug out the small flashlight from the backpack and began to sparingly use it. Yes she had another set of batteries, but she didn't know how long a set of batteries lasted in a flashlight. She had never used one continuously like she would this one. Still she tried to turn it on and off to conserve the batteries. But eventually she had no choice, to see she had to leave it on. And still the trail wound and twisted through the trees and mountains giving no hint to an end. She only had the tunnel of light with everything outside of that light not existing. It was the sound of the snow crunching under her feet and the light on the trail that became her only thoughts and her only world. She was finding, because of her shaking that she couldn't hold the light steady, but she refused to give up and continued to place one shaky foot in front of the other. Her hands were numb and her fingers stung – a dangerous sign, but there was little she could do about it. How far had she come? She really had no idea. It could have been a few feet, or it could have been miles. Her mind refused to focus on anything. She just walked, staying in the light, uphill, downhill, around the curves, through the twists and turns. Finally just staring and not even knowing what she was doing she just pushed ahead. To stop was to *die,* to move was to *live. And she so desperately wanted to live.*

She found herself clumsy and weaving on the trail as if she was drunk. And then she slipped and fell hard. It hurt! She had dropped her flashlight, looking for it she saw the light from it and fortunately the flashlight seemed undamaged. Crawling over to where it had landed she grabbed it, and then with much difficulty forced herself back onto her feet. She stood for a moment weaving, with little strength left in her legs, light headed and a little dizzy, thinking that she might end up right back on the snow. She leaned against a tree for support. For a moment or two she was disorientated, and wasn't quite sure which way was the right direction. She started off and then realized that there were tracks in the snow. When it registered she realized that she was going in the wrong direction, stopped, turned around and continued to fight for her life. Looking outside her narrow beam of light she saw that it was very dark. It seemed to her that there should be a full moon. At least that's what she remembered from this morning before the sun rose. But not knowing the time and when the moon would rise or how much the moon's light would penetrate this dark, silent, forest, all she could do was shake her head and continue.

The trail ahead of her within the light's beam seemed to be making a large left-hand sweep. It seemed so slight that she wasn't sure if it was just an illusion or if her mind was playing tricks on her. Yet it appeared to continue in this left direction . . . then before her opened a valley that lay below her, as she emerged from the forest. Even in her exhausted state she caught her breath at the beauty before her. The moon was out in its full glory, and yes the trees had blocked the light. The whole valley and pasture that lay below her was bathed in the soft moonlight making it appear to almost be surreal. Looking ahead and down she could see the trail she was on had a couple of tight switchbacks on it's way down the mountainside before it disappeared somewhere on the edge of that meadow. *Maybe, just maybe there will be something here that can provide me shelter.* It was a while before she realized that she was just standing there staring out at the scene below her. Shaking her head she slowly started out again being careful and not wanting to fall again. It seemed to be a long way down and thusly why the switchbacks in the trail. She felt that if she did fall that there would be a great chance she would never get up again. Plus falling here would be doubly dangerous. Her legs were now definitely rubber, and she could not stop the shaking and chattering of her teeth. Her breathing had become quite ragged, and she was close to tears. She was literally at the end. She was nearing the halfway point down the grade and could see where the trail entered the meadow when she stepped on a rock hidden in the snow, slipped, started falling, and screamed as she slid down the remaining hillside, gathering speed as she continued to fall. Then, as she hit the bottom, she was briefly aware that she had hurt something, but that was all, as consciousness slipped away from her, and she remembered nothing.

Wednesday – Hillstown Search and Rescue

Laura briefly came awake and thought back to last night. It had been an interesting one and the intimacy that she and Terry had shared had been wonderful. She rolled over to see if Terry was sleeping and saw that his side of the bed was empty. In her half sleep state she thought that this was one of the many things she had always loved about him. Very responsible, and caring, never shirking from what had to be done. Well the day was ahead of her in a couple of hours. With that she dug herself deeper under the warm covers and fell back to sleep.

* * *

The team was at the accident site just as the skies grayed from the coming day. With the days still being short they wanted to use every minute of available light to search. If nothing came out of their searching today then Terry would request an increase in the amount of people involved. He hoped to have this end today one way or the other. "Bob, if I remember right, we have a ridgeline that splits here; with the road on the north side and that narrow valley on the south. Does that sound about right?"

"Yes and the area to the south of that ridgeline runs west-south-west and away from the road. In fact it leads one pretty deep into the wilderness area. Let's see, I know that a ways in that you eventually will pick up the wilderness trail and that area where the trappers had been ambushed in the distant past. Truthfully there is no way once you start down in that direction to get back to the road. In fact had she been able to cross the stream to the east here she would have been able to find an easy way up to the road. But I understand the reluctance. The stream has always run fast, and with it being as cold as it has been, getting wet would be a sure way to get one killed."

They had ridden on just three snowmobiles riding double, with each carrying their backpacks and supplies. As everything they would work today would be on foot. Once he was on the scene of the accident he knew that there had been no exaggeration of what they faced from the report that Paul gave them the previous night. "Okay Paul, since you and Art were the ones who found this, lead us down to the wreck, if you please."

"Sure, no prob, just be prepared this isn't easy. By the way, I'm curious as to why we've left the other three snowmobiles at the trail head just outside of town."

"As Bob just stated, there is a wilderness trail that we will eventually tie into. And that's why I had us park the other three snowmobiles at the trailhead. I'm guessing that we will be able to push completely through that trail today. I want to cover the whole distance from here back to where the trail comes out. I know that it's a pretty good distance, probably somewhere around 20 miles. But I think with the six of us that we can cover that distance and do a decent job of searching."

"Okay TD, makes sense to me." Then heading over the side, Paul with Art assisting, led them into the tree line and berry bushes. Like the previous night it was a struggle to fight their way through and eventually be on the south side of the ridge. Following the struggle through the brush they approached the wrecked car. It was now light enough to see without the use of a flashlight. "I searched the car while Art searched the surrounding area." Then opening the rear door behind the driver seat he let them see what he had found. "You can see that she was at least smart enough to tear up the seats for additional warmth . . . And stay with the wreck through most of the storm. I'm guessing with the strength of this storm and the way it gave the appearance that it might break on Monday she decided to take her chances. It's really too bad she hadn't waited a little longer. Had she, well the two of us passed this area and she might have been able to yell or do something to catch our attention. Hey look there on the back shelf, it's her handi-talkie. Suspect she must have taken it out hoping and wishing to hear something."

" Really? Yeah and if wishes were money we'd all be rich." Bob responded.

They spread out and did a thorough search of the area. And like Art located the copse she had used for her needs. They continued looking for anything that would identify her direction. They knew that she couldn't go under the bridge that spanned the stream, but that didn't mean that couldn't have gone down stream in the opposite direction. From this point it seemed a very strong possibility. Still there was the note she had left stating she was going to try and get back on the road. So after some discussion it was decided to work their way down the ridgeline, as from their point of view that someone with little or no wilderness experience, that that direction would appear to give one the best possibility of getting back to the road. With the storm hitting the area with its final fury before leaving there was no sign at all as to her direction of travel, nothing to show her passing, it as if she never existed. So TD said a silent prayer asking that they be led in the necessary direction, and for them to have a successful outcome to this search and rescue. He had them divide up into the same two member teams and they spread out and began their search.

As the skies lightened and the early morning chill started to dissipate it appeared that finally the cold from that last storm was gone. With the rising of the sun there seemed to be a promise of a warmer day. In fact it was already becoming obvious that they would be removing some of the layers of clothing they were wearing, and placing them in their backpacks as they began to warm up. They could almost sense that spring was in the air. There was just a feeling to it that had been different when comparing yesterday to today. Yes, there was a chance that most likely the next two weekends might actually end the longer skiing season – a boon for the skiers as they would have an extended season this year. As they continued searching there still was nothing to show that she had passed this way. As midmorning approached they started to doubt that they were searching in the correct direction, b*ut no other direction made sense.* By late morning with no sign that she had passed this way they entered the first of many meadows that lay in the region. Here the meadow, because of the way the ridge ran went in a southerly direction before changing and heading more to the west. Still at this point there was nothing. Shaking his head TD was beginning to doubt that they were going right . . . but once again, nothing else made sense. "Look guys I want us all to spread out across the meadow. It's pretty wide so I need all of us to do a sweep here. Keep it close enough that we can see each other. I want to do this southern running portion first all the way to the edge. Then we'll come back and run the other portion that heads west."

They spread out and started out across the meadow when Bob yelled, "There's tracks here of what I suspect is wolves. There has been, in the near past, wolves reintroduced here. Let's hope they didn't find her. I'm sure this time of year that they would have no problem attacking a human for food since food would be pretty scarce."

This worried them all. It was a factor that they hadn't considered. Could she have been brought down by the pack? If she had it would have been a horrible way to die, a truly horrible way. With these thoughts they continued their search across the meadow. Then in the distance they could see a dark object lying in the snow. And the snow seemed to be tinged with a red color. Also the snow appeared to be churned up heavily as they came closer. TD hesitated hoping that what they saw wasn't the missing woman, but what else could it be? Bob reached the site ahead of the rest of the team, and from his body language it appeared that whatever it was wasn't the missing girl. But until TD reached the spot he'd hold his judgement. As he approached Bob said, "It appears that it was a deer, a doe I suspect. I suspect that the pack ran it out here in the open and then brought it down. Thankfully it didn't turn out to be our girl."

"You're telling me." TD said. "I almost hesitated coming over here thinking that it could be. How long ago do you think this happened?"

"A couple of days at the most", Bob said. "I suspect sometime Monday, but that's only a guess. The carcass has had time to freeze almost completely through, and with the blood on this snow it means that they came back to it after the storm ended. Truthfully, had it been much earlier, the carcass would have been too frozen for them to be able to work it as it has been."

"Okay then, let's spread back out work in this direction to the end of the meadow, and if we don't find anything meet back over there where the meadow makes that change in direction to the west and then we'll sweep it in that direction. I think that by the time we finish the other portion that we'll break for lunch. Bob, I know it's your area of expertise, but aren't we close to that wilderness trail?"

"Not as close as you think, but it's not too far from here. We still have to work our way around the edge of the hills over there and then to the edge of this same large meadow." He pointed out the direction he was speaking. "Once there I think we are close to the area where those trappers met their fate. Of course there are a number of meadows that the trail works itself through before we reach the trail head – besides running long distances under the canopy of the trees. "

"Okay all, let's finish this sweep and then break for lunch." Thinking about this portion of the meadow he knew that it first went in the southerly direction that they had just searched. Back at the tree line it then continued west where it went against a hillside and then proceeded south again. The topography here was such that it funneled the winds straight into the meadows. Again, if his memory was correct, sometime in the great past there had been a blow down of a portion of the trees. It had appeared, in one's imagination, as some giant, angry about something, had just come in and leveled the area, piling the trees haphazardly, and allowing them to lie as they fell. The winds that had done this damage must have been unbelievable. When you looked at some of the trunks of these dead and downed trees you could tell that some were at least 100 years old. While it had happened a long time in the past he was glad he hadn't been here when it had transpired.

Once again they spread out and began their searching. As the approached the pile of dead trees excitement grabbed at their very souls. Right before them at the blow down were tracks in the snow. Immediately they knew that what they were seeing wasn't tracks of animals but of a person. The tracks were small and could be tracks of either an older child or a woman. Now, with the finding of these tracks, lunch took a back seat. "I need one of you smaller guys to crawl into the blow down and see if there is something that will help identify these tracks as the one we are looking for." Shrugging TD continued. "I mean I am very hopeful, but with our luck it could turn out to be a wilderness survivalist who was here." The two assistants to Art and Reggie volunteered, and the two then began a slow crawl into that massive tangle, while the remainder remained outside. "Jacob, while we are waiting, follow these tracks out on the meadow here and see where they go. When you reach the cliff edge, overlooking that valley, then return and let us know what you have found."

"Okay, Paul why don't you come with me. I know it's easy to follow the tracks in the snow, but if I reach a point where the snow is gone I think having a tracker with me would be a good idea."

The two of them headed off to the south following the tracks that lay before them while Bob and TD waited for the report of the two who were crawling inside the pile of dead and downed trees. Finally one of the two yelled out, after having directed his buddy to a location somewhere in the center. "TD, Bob, someone has camped here. There is a remainder of a fire here. From the amount of ash I would guess that someone spent at least a day here. From the way this was built I would guess that no survivalist would have done it this way. This was definitely built by someone with no experience. I'd say they were lucky they didn't set the whole thing on fire. There's a lot of stirred up dirt and the grasses have been pulled up. From both the size of the footprints and the prints left where the person took a leak my guess is we are talking about a woman. Because of the low roof in here a guy would take a leak on his knees while a girl would be crouching on her feet using the downed trees or a branch for support. I think we have found where she spent the night. As cold as the ashes are she has been gone from here . . . oh I'd say since probably yesterday morning. We're on our way out. Other than a campsite there's nothing else here."

"Bob, if I remember it right, yesterday was an extremely cold day. If she left her shelter early in the day and continued, well you know where I am going with this. I don't think she was properly dressed to handle the cold. While this is a positive sight here, we still haven't found her, and she has over a twenty-four hour lead on us. Do you know of any area similar to this that she would have been able to get into to protect herself last night?"

Thinking about it for a little while Bob shook his head saying, "No. The meadow up ahead is open for primitive camping, but once you leave that you pick up that wilderness trail, and it goes for a great distance under the trees, but there's nothing that would get one out of the elements at all. The trail winds and twists through the mountains to give one both a good hike and to give hikers some of the great views that this area has. After all, it's purpose it not just to get from point "A" to point "B", but to make it both challenging and interesting."

"Hey, TD!" Jacob yelled, as he and Paul returned to the group. "This person and we now believe that it was a woman because of the stride, and from Paul's evaluation, one with little or no experience. So I would say this probably is our missing girl. Go ahead Paul and tell them what you told me."

"It's just that the way she stopped at the stream ahead, and I would guess it was so she could fill her water containers, speaks loudly of a tenderfoot. I immediately noticed that there were two or three other points along that stream where it would have been far safer and easier to do that. Where she filled her containers there was a great chance of falling into that icy water. My guess is she went by here, by the condition of her tracks in the snow, sometime yesterday morning."

Looking at Bob as they awaited the other two to emerge from the piled trees TD said. "Well that confirms it I guess. The two that went into the deadfall said just about the same thing. So we have it now confirmed from two different sources that this is a woman, and one who has no experience. This has to be our accident victim. She must be a pretty strong person to have accomplished everything she has so far. Or the Lord is watching out for her."

"Now don't bring your God into this." Bob said. "My guess is, yes she is strong, but I chalk it up to luck. But we haven't found her yet, and there's still a great possibility that in the end, all we will end up with is a body – another one of the many who have died of exposure out here."

"True. Look let's take a quick break and grab something to eat. We need the energy to continue anyway." Pausing for a second, TD continued. "We'll take no more than 15 minutes and then head out. With the tracks we have it will be easier for us to follow." The team took time to put some food away. Those calories would be needed with the distance still to go.

While it was warming, as the day progressed, and there was a sense of the coming spring it was still very cold, and they knew that to just keep warm required a lot of energy. They idly talked about many different things as conversations usually go. "I wonder who this woman is?" Paul asked.

"What do you mean?" Bob asked.

"Well if I have this right she has no outdoor or wilderness experience. In fact from what little I have gathered she is a flatlander royal. One who would prefer just to drive through an area such as this, return and remain in the cities . . . Wants nothing at all to do with this style of life. So how is that she has survived, at least up to here? That storm was fierce. It easily could have been one of our mid-winter types of storms. After all, she survived two nights in that wreck, and then left, trying to get back. Yeah I know it was stupid, but then during some of the strongest winds and heavy snowfall she finds shelter here. I suspect that she may even have come close to facing that pack. Yet, here is the proof she was alive at least at the time she left here. I know that we have no idea if she still is, but if she has done this well . . . well who is she?"

"A good question really, now that you have put it that way. I would say that she probably has a stubborn streak. It would take that to fight through this and obviously some inner steel. Something she may not even have known that she had. Sometimes a person doesn't even know what they have until they have to face something like this. You know something that takes them completely out of their comfort zone, and places them in a life or death situation." Silent for a moment Bob continued. "TD both you and I have seen men die from less than this. Some of them just fold up and giving up . . . Yeah Paul a very good question."

Interrupting TD said. "Enough guys, let's move. There's much ahead of us and we truthfully do not know if she found the trail that lies over at the end of this meadow area. It is something that could be easily missed."

With the tracks ahead of them they began to follow the trail left by Cathy. Thanks to the snow it was an easy trail to follow, as hers were the only tracks in the fresh snow. As they worked through the area and to the edge of the meadow they could see that she had kept to the tree line on her left as if she was attempting to find a way to go in that direction. By doing this she was going to come across the trail. So they were almost sure that she probably had taken it. As it would make sense even to a tenderfoot that a trail had to lead somewhere. And sure enough as they came to the point where the trail entered the meadow the tracks continued. Watching they could see where the tracks continued and disappeared in the distance on the trail. They could see that she had brushed the snow off the plaque identifying the tragedy that happened here in the early 1800's. Everything, timewise pointed to yesterday – a day that had been severely cold, actually colder than when the storm had been active, making it more than a possibility that one could go down from exposure. How far did she get, and was she still alive? This was the question that was weighing heavily on all their minds now, and if the truth be told, they were beginning to respect this unknown woman. Here, obvious to them, was one who would not give up and would continue to fight. One who, obvious to them now, had a huge inner strength, and while probably was scared beyond anything she had ever faced, still pushed on. There had been so many others in the past that had faced less and never survived. Now and silently they all began to push for this woman, to hope that she persevered, and they knew that somewhere ahead were the answers. They all wanted to find her alive, and to see who this woman was that had conquered what others had not.

Unconsciously the team picked up their pace. They knew every second that they saved might mean that there was a chance for her survival. But, at the same time knowing that from what they knew of the area where she presently might be located, that there was no place to stop – no shelter of any kind. Yes, further along there were some cabins. But those were a great distance away. They doubted that she had the strength and endurance to cover the distance to get to those cabins. Yet even if she had, yes even if she did reach those cabins, most were summer cabins and were abandoned during the winter months. Once one was in these cabins during the winter months you were there for the whole winter, unless one wanted to hike out or had a working snowmobile. There was no access until the snows melted and the old logging roads were reopened into the area. So thinking the worst and hoping for the best they pushed themselves harder.

Cathy – Wednesday

She slowly awakened finding herself lying in a bed warm and comfortable. She was covered in layers of blankets and was still in the twilight that one knows – kind of the state of being awake and yet falling back to sleep. She heard the crackling of a fire, but where she was and where it was located seemed very distant. Drowsily she drifted out again. As she fell back to sleep she wondered idly if everything she had gone through was just a dream. Then sleep took her and she remembered nothing.

Turning from his chair he had witnessed the brief waking of his patient. "Well Sam I guess it will be a little while yet before we can be introduced." Then turning back to his writing he continued to work. Spring would be here soon, and he, for one, was eager to get off the mountain. While he knew that what he did was necessary, by the time spring arrived he was quite fed up playing the hermit. As Wednesday continued towards noon he continued to watch this woman wondering how she had ended up where she did in the first place. Very rarely did he see anybody out this way this time of year, and it was a surprise when he found her. Thinking back to last night he remembered sitting by the fireplace just sort of relaxing and not thinking about much at all. So far this winter he had finished another manuscript and knew that the hard work was still ahead of him. He hated the revising part, but knew that it was this part of the writing that required the most discipline and that which made his manuscripts sellable. He figured that this last storm which had just left was probably the end of winter's grip.

Staring out the window on the magical scene of a full moon, on the pasture that lay just outside of his cabin, he was enjoying the quiet and the beauty of God's world. The solitude here let him fully concentrate on his writings. Completely relaxed he noticed that suddenly Sam jumped up and was alert. Curious he got up and then opened the front door that faced the meadows. Sam seemed eager to go out which was unusual for this time of the night. The dog seemed to be content to lie by the fire until later when they both would go out for a short period. He remembered asking Sam. "What is it boy?" The dog looked up at him questioningly as if he should have known. It was then he heard the scream, and then nothing. At least that's what it sounded like. But it could have been some animal. Yet Sam wasn't acting like it was an animal. So getting his heavy coat on, then putting on his hat and gloves, and boots, he grabbed his flashlight, not that he needed it with the full moon, and both he and Sam headed out to investigate.

Really not sure where the sound had come from he headed out into the meadow area, and was invigorated by the cold fresh air. It really woke him up from the relaxed state he had been in. This meadow area was huge, and thinking back to the sound of that scream, he realized that it came from some distance away. So most likely he could begin looking when he was well into the meadow. Sam was on the alert and seemed to be heading straight across, barking now and then as if to say come this way and follow me. Shrugging he thought that maybe it would be a good idea to begin the search on the far side. That way he would be working his way back to the cabin, and wouldn't be retracing any steps. He found that the cold was starting to penetrate his clothing now and it was colder than he thought. So he picked up his pace and suddenly the dog began to bark excitedly like he had found something. So yelling he said, "Okay boy, I'm coming. What is it that you found?" He could barely make out Sam, but whatever it was that Sam could see said that it something that really had his interest. As he got closer he saw what looked like a pile of trash or rags from a distance. As he got closer there also seemed to be a backpack in that pile. He wondered how this had gotten here, as it was an area that he walked quite frequently. Then the pile moved, and there was a soft moan that came from it.

Stopping for a moment he realized that what he had mistaken as a pile of trash was a person. Picking up his pace he joined Sam, and crouched down and was further surprised, as this person was a woman. *A woman? What the heck is she doing out here?* Well there was not the time to question this. If she had remained out here unconscious, as she presently seemed to be, then she would be dead by morning. Carefully as he could he picked her up and with this additional burden he headed back to the cabin. He had taken off her backpack and put it on to make it easier to carry her. She seemed to be dressed somewhat strangely, but with the soft moonlight he could be mistaken. It took him a while to finally get back to the cabin, as he had to put her down a couple of times to catch his breath. Finally getting back inside the cabin he put her initially on the bed. Feeling her skin he saw that she probably was near death from the cold anyway so he needed to move and get her warm. Again, curious about the way she was dressed, it almost seemed that she was wearing . . . well wearing car seat material? But if she had been involved in an accident – again the main road through the area was miles from here – how'd she get here? He moved her over close to the fire so that the heat could help warm her. Carefully, since he did not know the extent of her injuries, he began to remove this makeshift covering she had on.

The first thing he discovered was that there was ice between her and this stuff. She must have been sweating at some point, and once she cooled then the sweat became ice. He needed to undress her and get her in the bed. And once this was accomplished he would get some of the stones he used for warming heated up and placed close to her in bed. He knew that there was still a good chance that she could die unless her body's core was warmed. He worked rapidly and carefully, not wanting to injure her more, but finally had her stripped down to her underwear and bra. Most of what she was wearing was either wet or had ice forming. He noticed that she had bruises over portions of her body, and a very swollen ankle. She was extremely cold and her breathing was shallow. He quickly put her into the bed and heaped layers of blankets on her. He followed this by carefully climbing in to add his body heat temporarily to get her warm. He eventually heard the water boiling, and knew that his round stones were now heated. So climbing out he grabbed the towels he used to wrap the stones, did so, and then placed the warm stones against her.

From the brief inspection he had made of her his conclusion was that she was a pretty young thing . . .

Couldn't be much older than her middle 20's. She seemed to be quite dirty, but considering what she had been through this was no surprise. Now all he could do was to continue to rotate the stones to help her gain her body heat back, and pray. Still shaking his head he kept asking himself, how'd she get here? Being a Christian, he prayed for her recovery and for half the night he continued to change the stones. Finally she seemed to be warm, and also seemed to be resting much easier. At this point for her comfort he removed the stones, built the fire up and then banked it. There was a cot he kept that was rarely used so he used it for this night. Sam lay by the fire, but kept his eyes on this woman. As if saying, I am watching, you go ahead and sleep, and sleep he did.

The next morning, as he had worked around the cabin, there had been little or no movement from his patient until that brief awakening around midmorning. Poor girl had obviously been at the end when she fell. In his mind he could see, in the moonlight, where she had slipped and then fallen down the hillside to end up where she had. Shortly he hoped to have some of his questions answered, but knew that it might be a while before she could really be up to answering questions.

As noon approached he finally saw some stirring that might reflect that she was waking. Sitting at the table he watched as she slowly stretched, yawned, and opened her eyes. The first thing he saw in those eyes was questioning, then a little fear, as she looked around.

* * *

Cathy, as she awoke, wondered where she was, then stretching she yawned. She was comfortable and warm, and yet much of her body hurt. Where she was now was no place she had ever been, and that brought a little fear to her. Then she saw a man sitting at a table looking at her. He had a full beard, and his hair was shoulder length. He easily could have come right out of the 1800's. She then noticed a dog that was close to the fireplace watching her. The next thing she realized was that she was wearing next to nothing. *What's going on here?* How did she get here, and why was she almost naked? Staring briefly at the man she began to ask, but realized that she had no voice. He smiled at her and said, "Ah I see you are finally awake. Let me get you something hot to drink, and I guess before that some water to help clear your throat. You know you came close to dying last night. If Sam here hadn't heard something and wanted to investigate, you probably would have."

"Would have what?" she croaked

"You would have died out there from exposure. You had fallen and were unconscious when we found you. You were close to death then, and I can see in your eyes you are wondering why you are almost naked, and if anything happened that shouldn't have. Do I have that about right?" He had gotten up and went out of her sight returning with a glass of water which he handed to her, and he went back to the table. She nodded, signaling him to continue. You were very cold when we got you back here. I am guessing from what you were wearing that you were involved in a crash somewhere. But as I removed some of what you wore there was an ice layer that had built up between the layers you were wearing, and everything below that ice that you wore was damp – furthering the possibility that you could still lose your battle with the cold, and die right here. I had no choice I had to strip you down to what you have now, and then put you into the bed, and I actually had to get in with you for a short time to add my body heat to yours. At least until then stones got warmed up, at which time I put the warm stones against your body, and rotated them. Eventually you warmed up, and finally, from my eyes, were more comfortable and looked more like you were now sleeping normally. My guess is that you have been out close to 18 hours. I've gotten your real clothes dry so when you are ready to move, I'll step outside to give you some privacy. Then we can talk. It's actually lunchtime so I'll go ahead and fix us something. At that point you can fill me in on what happened, and I'll answer any of your questions. Fair? Oh by the way my name is Will Fellows, and yours is . . .?"

"Oh sorry, I'm Cathy Jahnsen, and yeah, okay, this is almost too much to take in. But I would feel better if I had more clothes on, so if you would, I will get dressed. Then you can direct me to the bathroom. I am sure I look like a complete mess right now."

"Considering what you went through and where it almost ended, I think you look pretty good really. Okay, I'm heading out the door. Do you want me to take Sam also?"

"Sam, who's Sam? Is there somebody else here?"

Laughing a little he said, "No, no one other than my dog. He keeps me company during these winter months. Sam, come on we need to give this lady some privacy. Soon as you get dressed the bathroom is right behind you through that door. When you are done, come out and let us know and we'll come in a get that meal going, and we can talk, okay? Oh by the way your stuff is hanging there by the fireplace so that they would dry out. Probably warm too." He then smiled at her, opened the door that led outside and with the dog left.

What an unexpected change of events, when she had fallen the only thing she could remember that had flashed in her mind was *no, not now*. And it appeared that she was safe and for once completely warm. Now what? Did she trust what this man said? Yet what other choice did she have? After all if he had wanted to take advantage of her he could have. But he didn't, so maybe he was exactly who he said he was. Glancing once more to make sure she was alone inside the cabin she threw the covers off of her, and immediately regretted moving so quickly. She hurt, and it seemed to be just about everywhere. She then gingerly swung her legs over the edge of the bed and tried to stand only to fall back on the bed. She then looked at her ankle and saw that it was swollen, with angry red areas plus black and blue splotches. She really had twisted that one in the fall. She also found that the brief standing she had done left her light headed, dizzy, and shaky. So this time carefully she braced herself as she stood up. She found that she couldn't put any weight on that foot at all. So she kind of hopped and hobbled over to the fireplace grabbed her clothes and then slowly and with care worked her way into the bathroom.

Once she was inside, she noticed that it was very small, having a toilet, sink and small shower, and nothing more. Surprising to her was the cleanliness of the place. After all a male lived here during the winter, and from her experience most were not so interested in keeping things neat and clean. First she took care of nature's call, and thought that it was nice to have a real toilet to use instead of trying to figure out how to make it work in the outdoors. Then staring at the shower stall she thought, *I've just got to take a shower.* Being out like she had been for the four to five days without such a convenience made this small shower stall look like a luxury. Before deciding whether she would or not she looked into the mirror over the sink and that made the decision for her. Her hair was a tangled mess, and seemed quite dirty and actually seemed to have sticks and such tangled in it. There were streaks of dirt and she suspected charcoal from the fires she had been close to on her face. Then looking at her body closer she saw the many bruises, cuts and contusions that seemed to have no end. Well if nothing else to feel clean would be a spiritual lift for her. So she turned on the water in the shower, waited for it to get hot, finished stripping down and climbed in. How could she describe the sensation? It wasn't like she had never taken a shower, but to take one after the ordeal she had just experienced made her appreciate something so simple. She kept it as hot as she could, trying to wash off the last few days of her trial. She found that the water stung her many small injuries, and burned her twisted ankle. But it felt great! Still she had to admit that she had learned much from this experience that she had just lived through.

This got her to wondering if God had had a hand in her journey. After all, what were the chances, with her inexperience, to have lived through what she had just experienced? It seemed that at every point when she needed shelter or protection that it had been there. Never obvious, but still it had been found just when she was at the end of what she could endure. This was something she would need to think about and try to understand. Right now she just hurt too much to be able to concentrate on anything. So instead she just enjoyed the hot spray from the shower. Finally she had to get out as her skin was wrinkling from being under the spray. Opening the door she found a couple of towels and dried off her body and used the second to wrap her wet hair. My, it felt good to be clean again. Limping over to the mirror she removed the towel from her hair, wiped off the fogged mirror, and tried with little success to put her hair in some semblance of order. She realized that unfortunately she had nothing clean to change into so went ahead and put her dirty clothes back on. Well, she still had to make compromises. Again having to be careful because of her injuries and soreness of her muscles it took her a while to be fully dressed again. Finally she emerged, and then jumped slightly as she had forgotten that he was here, and that he had come back into the cabin.

Seeing her jump and the grimace he came over to her and said, "Careful there, your ankle is in bad shape. I don't think it's broken, but it is a very bad sprain. Here let me help you over to the table. I think I have some crutches out in storage here." As he prepared to help her over to the table he noticed how she looked and said. "Well look at you, you clean up real nice there. I would never have been able to compare the girl that I carried in here last night to the one standing in front of me now." He then smiled an encouraging smile before continuing. "You know I suspect that there's a search and rescue team out looking for you right now. Okay here put your arm around my neck, and I'll put mine around your waist. Now lean on me and then you can sit at the table. I heard the shower going so I knew it was safe to come back inside – Should have thought about the crutches. I always have them here, as I am isolated during the winter months and sometimes I do something stupid and need them. Anyway I've got some food cooking, so please just sit and relax. Look you're shaking, please sit it's obvious that you don't have the strength yet to remain standing long."

She had to agree with just about everything he had said, and thankful for the assistance they made their way to the table where she thankfully sat back down. She hadn't realized just how weak she was, and she found that another wave of overwhelming fatigue was threatening her. "Thank you; do you have some coffee or something? I'm just about asleep again. You said that I've already slept 18 hours? I shouldn't be tired, but have to admit that I am." She then folded her arms on the table and put her head there. She really couldn't remember being so tired, even when she had crammed for finals in some of her college classes. She had remembered a couple of all nighters. Yet even then she hadn't felt as exhausted as she did now. She looked up and before her was a cup of steaming coffee. When did that get there? She then realized that she must have dozed off. Shaking her head she said. "I seem to be totally beat, sorry."

"Not surprising really. But let the coffee do its work, and then eat this stew, both should help. Then if you want to sleep some more please do. I think it is something that will help you heal faster anyway. So no more conversation, just eat. Then I'll help you back over to the bed."

Thankful for not having to either talk or think she drank the coffee and it was really good. Then he placed a bowl of stew in front of her with some baking powder biscuits, and then grabbed some for himself. He sat across from her and with some concern in his voice said, "Come on Cathy eat the stew. I'm sure that you've not had much in the last day or so and your body is going to need this to heal."

It took almost all of her effort just to nod her head. Then she tasted the stew and found it very good like the coffee. It had potatoes, vegetables, and plenty of meat. The broth was delicious, but she could not quite tell what had been used to give it the unique flavor she had tasted. She found that once she started that indeed she was hungry and thought that one bowl would not be enough. Yet as she finished it she found that she felt quite full. That was a surprise to her. She thought that because of the lack of food that she would just about devour everything in sight. She looked up questioningly, but before she could ask anything he spoke.

Smiling he said, "Cathy you have to think that for the last however many days that you've been eating a lot less than you normally would. So your stomach has shrunk. There's just not a lot of room down there right now. I can see that you can barely keep your eyes open. Here, let me help you back to the bed, and then when you wake back up I think you will want something more to eat. Shall we?" He got up from the chair and came over to her where she gratefully allowed him to help her back to the bed. Who was this man anyway? Well she wasn't going to get any answers now – she was almost asleep by the time her head hit the pillow.

Shaking his head and smiling Will covered her back up and then went to clean up from the meal they had just shared. She really had been lucky to survive. Then thinking about it maybe it wasn't luck after all. He knew that God had a tendency to work in ways that would never be understood. He knew that this girl was not an outdoorsman, and had no skills to survive in the wild. Yet she did. She had been out in the fury of that storm that could have brought down the most experienced, and yet she survived. As he continued to think about it he knew that even he being here to finally rescue her was not an accident. Had the storm not happened or had been mild, there would have been a good chance that he would have headed out – sick of being alone, and ready to catch up on all that he missed by locking himself away for the winter. He was definitely beginning to see the hand of God in this one. Shaking his head he whispered, "I wonder what God has in store for you my lady, I really wonder."

Search and Rescue – Late Wednesday Afternoon

The tracks left by Cathy were very visible in the snow. They saw that she had stuck to the trail. They also saw that she had stumbled and fell a number of times. Still it was difficult to know how far ahead of them she might be. There was still a great worry that now and soon they would come upon her body. They really did not know how this inexperienced person had gotten this far, but she had. Shaking his head Paul said, "TD, I don't understand it. This is a woman with absolutely not experience. How come she has at least survived to this point when others who did have the experience have perished? It just doesn't make any sense."

Smiling TD said. "Now Paul maybe it's because she doesn't know any better and maybe it's her inner strength, but I think I see the hand of the divine at work here. Besides just looking at this, would you want to cross this woman? I mean here she has beaten the odds on living through this – I know at least to this point. But still with this kind of strength and stubbornness I think she would be a real firebrand in a discussion."

Laughing Bob said. "Discussion huh, I think you mean a disagreement or fight right? I can see that you are a married man, not that we didn't know that, but you chose your words carefully there."

"Take it any way you would like Bob, but this girl has shown us something that's for sure. We only have a few hours of daylight left shall we continue? How far are we from that meadow anyway?"

"I'd guess at least an hour, probably closer to two. Suspect we'll reach it at dusk. Do you think that she made it that far?" Paul asked.

Shrugging TD said, "Don't really know. But I do know that on the far side of that large meadow is where Will spends his winters, and then once past there we have about 5 miles before we reach the trailhead and where half of our snowmobiles are parked. So even with the pace we are keeping it will be dark by the time we are out of here."

"Will . . . Will who?" Paul asked

"Oh the writer . . . You know the one who spends his winters up here in his cabin. He told me it was the only place he could go to get away from distractions and to put together his manuscripts. His cabin is in the Westland Tract. I think there are about 4 or 5 cabins located there. But he is the only one that's up there during the winter. As you know most are occupied only in the summer months, but I just remembered that Will spends his winters in his."

Silent for a moment Bob asked. "So do you think that she got that far?"

"We can only hope, and then hope that he's still there. This is the time of year that he normally heads out. Always says that by the time winter is close to over that he is done, finished and ready to face the real world again. He may have just closed shop and headed out for all that I know. Anyway, standing here is not getting either her found or us out of here, let's go." They pushed on, as the short days were a hindrance, all of them having to admit that no matter what the outcome they all had respect for this lost woman – all of them silently wishing that she would be found alive, and not one who would have succumbed to the conditions. As they continued along the trail following her tracks they could see the fatigue there. There seemed to be more stopping to rest, and again more stumbling. The trail she left was beginning to show more wandering and weaving a sure sign that she was all done in. They expected at any time now to find her dead. How far could she go anyway? Everything pointed to an unhappy ending, yet in their minds no matter how it ended she had their respect.

It was approaching dusk when they hit the trail where it switch-backed down into the meadow. Carefully they proceeded, still following her tracks. Then before them they saw heavily disturbed snow and scrape over the side and nothing. The tracks had ended right here. Puzzled, in the failing light, they stopped and searched but found nothing. There were no tracks of animals or such that could have attacked her, just an ending of her tracks. "Okay Paul", Bob asked, "you're the tracker here, what do you think happened?"

He shrugged, and for the moment he shook his head. He initially was at a loss. "Don't know . . . I guess we need to go a little further along, maybe the story will unfold for us." With nothing else to make a judgement by, they continued on, in the failing light, down the trail and through the switchbacks heading towards the meadows below. "You know what . . . I think she fell at that point. It's the only thing that makes any sense. Now if we find a body at the bottom all I can say is poor girl. To be so close and then not make it . . ." He trailed off, as they all knew what he had been thinking, but none of them wanted to put it into words. With care they finally reached the base of the hill and were standing on the edge of the meadow. With flashlights out now they began to search the area attempting to line up the disturbance they had found above with where they presently were. The trail had come out into the meadow to the north of where she had apparently fallen.

"Look, there are tracks of an animal coming across the meadow going in that direction." Bob said as he pointed to the south. "I wonder . . ."

"Wonder what Bob?" Jacob asked. He had remained quiet through most of the search, but now was curious as to what Bob had been thinking. After all animal tracks out here wouldn't be that unusual. Especially since the storm had broken and no new snow had fallen to cover any tracks.

"Guys what if those tracks belonged to ah, what was his name, Will's dog. You did say he had one didn't you TD?"

"No, I don't think I mentioned a dog, but yes he does have one. So do you want to follow these tracks is that it?"

"Yeah, from what I can see they are heading in the direction we want to go anyway." They then picked up the tracks and followed them. They saw that whatever animal it was, wasn't wandering aimlessly around but making almost a straight line towards something. Shortly they found another set of tracks these belonging to possibly a man from the size of the print and the stride, and they too were heading in the same direction. Finally the two sets of tracks intersected and headed towards the hillside that they had just come down from. When they reached the bottom of the hill they found a larger area of messed up snow. The tracks they had followed led them here and once there the tracks became a jumble. Here the snow had been knocked down to the frozen earth and dead grasses that lay below. Then the tracks headed generally west, and while it wasn't real obvious it appeared that whoever this was was now carrying a burden of some kind. As they followed these new tracks leading away from this point they could see that the animal tracks were right beside whoever this was. Then they found the first place where he stopped and had placed his bundle on the snow to take a break.

Excited now, since it seemed that maybe this bundle he was carrying had some weight and forced him to rest. "Well TD, Jacob, Bob, what do you think? I'm beginning to have at least a little hope. My guess is he's carrying her. I suspect that she did indeed fall, and was at least knocked unconscious. If she had died I would guess that he would have left her there, gone back to find something to put her body in, and then would have brought it back at that time. My gut feeling here is, at the moment of discovery she was alive so he needed to work quickly thusly the one set of tracks out and so far the one set of tracks back. TD have you ever been to his cabin?"

"No, not directly, but I've been out to the tract a few times and understand his was the one furthest east and isolated in comparison to the other cabins, actually the first one to face this meadow here. But I have to agree with you. Even with his burden he was trying to make some time. Well let's assume that he found her, and then let's just head to the western edge here, kind of generally following the tracks. It's close to dark and we need to move anyway." They picked up the pace and shortly in the distance saw light coming from a window. With this light as a guide they quickly covered the distance only to find Will outside waiting for them. Sitting next to him was his dog. He raised his hand and waved at them, which they returned. "Guys, be quiet please. I assume that you are the search and rescue team out trying to find the missing girl. Sam here heard you long before I did, but from his reaction I knew that there had to be someone approaching the cabin, so I came out to meet you."

"Will, are you sure you're not out of the 1800's? With that full beard and long hair all you are missing is the leather outfits they used to wear and of course the hat." Jacob said.

Laughing a little Will said. "Yeah that's the way of it when you spend the winter alone. Your missing girl is safe. She's sleeping right now. I don't know how she made it this far, but if I hadn't been here she would have died over there. She had fallen and was unconscious. In the fall she had hurt her ankle severely, not broken, but almost impossible to walk on anyway. She's completely wiped out, and right now sleep is something she really needs. So I didn't want you all to come here being noisy and wake her up. I suspect in the morning that she'll be more herself. My cabin is small but I think I can put you guys up for the night if you want to stay. TD why don't you go in and check on her while the rest of us waits out here. Then you can confirm that she's okay."

Nodding TD quietly entered the cabin and in the corner saw the bed and Cathy sleeping. He went over to the bed and saw that she appeared to be resting peacefully and seemed to be okay. He quietly left and went back outside. Smiling he said, "She looks good for having to go through what she did. As for spending the night I don't think there's room enough. We'll head out and back to town. I'm going to inform dispatch so they can let the families know, and then tomorrow we'll be back with the snowmobiles to pick her up. She'll get a free ride in one of the sleds that we will attach and then she can be checked out at the hospital after a brief ambulance ride, and then I guess back home."

"Well your call TD, but I've had nobody around all winter and it's kind of nice to have someone to talk to other than Sam here. But I know I'm about done here for this season anyway. I'm sure she'll be eager to see your face tomorrow, knowing now for sure that her ordeal is over. Do me a favor though. I suspect she would like something clean to wear out of here. I kind of hand wash everything and it works fine for me, but wouldn't work with her stuff. Hold on a minute and I'll get what she isn't wearing, you take it home to your wife and I'm sure she won't mind washing and drying the clothes. Then when you show up tomorrow you can present her with her clean clothes."

* * *

When Cathy awoke the next morning a number of things hit her all at once. First she noticed that she was still in her clothes. Thinking about that she realized that the last time she had done something like this, other than through this ordeal she had just survived, was when she was eleven years old and had gone out with the family to a theme park where she had run all day. Coming home that night she remembered going into her bedroom, lying on the bed thinking about the fun she had that day, and then woke up the next morning never even realizing that she had fallen asleep. Then, as is usual, it was her full bladder that had awakened her. Looking around she saw a pair of crutches close by for her use, and she realized that she was starving. Looking towards the table where she had sat the previous day she saw sunlight hitting it. The scene seemed so relaxing and normal. Remembering that she hurt just about everywhere she gingerly worked herself to a sitting position then reached and grabbed for the crutches. She smelled the beginnings of breakfast being cooked. These smells were just beginning to permeate the cabin and immediately made her tummy rumble. Then she, with care, stood up and saw Will standing at the stove with his back to her cooking the meal. He said, cheerfully, "Ah I see you're finally moving. Thought you might wake up soon, and if you hadn't I probably would have gotten you up anyway. You see last night . . ."

She interrupted him at this point and said, "Sorry Will, but I've got to make my trip to the bathroom. Once I'm back out you can fill me in, and a big cup of coffee would be very nice."

Smiling at her, he just waved her on and turned back to the food he was preparing. She went into the bathroom, took care of her needs, and followed this by standing in front of the mirror. She still felt like she looked like death warmed over. Running her fingers through her hair she thought, this is going to take forever to untangle and get right. She washed her hands and with the use of the crutches, limped back out and over to the table and sat down. She was finding that even with all the rest she had she still felt tired and weak. There at the table, as she had requested, was a large cup of coffee. Shortly what followed were pancakes, ham, and what appeared to be scrambled eggs.

"I'm sorry about the eggs, but with the time I spend up here I can't keep fresh eggs. So these are powdered eggs. The rest isn't much of a problem, I've just never figured out how to keep fresh eggs up here through the winter. So eat up and I won't be offended if you don't eat the eggs. Okay, as I was just about to say when you needed to use the facilities was that yesterday, actually towards evening, when you were quite dead to this world, the rescue team arrived. The leader is our local Sheriff known as TD. He'll be back here sometime this morning to pick you up and take you out of here and then eventually home. From what I have gathered they want you to go to the hospital to make sure your injuries are just minor, and with this I concur. Also, I hope you don't mind but I sent some of your dirty clothes with him so that you would have something clean to wear when you left here. I understand that he called dispatch last night, and your family now knows that you are well. Unfortunately there is no way for you to talk to them from here. So this brings you up to date, and unfortunately that's all I have for you."

Silent, as she took it all in, she found that suddenly the tears started flowing unbidden. She suddenly realized that it was finally over and that she was safe and soon would be home again. Through the tears she said, "Sorry, it's not you. But finally . . . finally I know that it's over. And I think everything that I've been holding in . . ." Then she couldn't speak as the tears continued to flow. He came around the table and offered her a hug, which she gratefully accepted. Leaning on him and holding tightly she continued to cry. Eventually she could feel the flow of emotion and tears begin to diminish, and found that once again she was drained, but was actually feeling better. She slowly let go and carefully sat back down. He handed her something she could use to blow her nose and wipe her face. It was truly over. She finished her food, and actually asked for some more. When finished with the food she had another large cup of coffee. Now that she seemed full and relaxed her curiosity came to the surface. "Okay Will, I must admit that when I awoke the first time you scared me to death. After all, where do you find someone with a full beard and hair down to his shoulders like that these days except in those scary movies where one looking like you is the bad guy? So why do you do this?"

This led to a conversation of what he did for a living and why he had found that it was necessary for him to do this every year, and that he was a Christian who also wrote Christian stories along with the other genres. The time flowed past and before she knew it she could hear a couple of snowmobiles approaching and knew now, for sure, that she was on her way home. Excitement began to grow within her as she contemplated the reunion with both her family and with Keith. After all, their planned wedding would be only a few months off, and now she would be there. Something she hadn't been sure of since finding herself in that accident on Saturday. Then she heard them pull up and the machines went quiet. She heard two people approaching the door and with Will saying, "Come on in, don't worry about knocking. Everyone's decent and our guest is waiting to be introduced."

Through the door came two men, the taller of the two had the uniform of the county sheriff, and the shorter just something that appeared to be comfortable. Smiling, she said, "Hi I'm Cathy, and please excuse me if I don't get up to greet you."

The sheriff responded by saying, "Pleased to make your acquaintance Cathy, I'm Terry or TD as this is what the locals call me and the one standing next to me is Jacob. He and his wife have a small dairy outside of town." Then looking down at the bag he was carrying he continued. "This is for you. As you probably are aware Will here gave us some of your dirty clothes to wash. Last night Laura, that's my wife, went ahead and washed, dried, and then folded them. I think you'll find a little treat in there also. She said that after one had been through what you had that you deserved to be babied. I think she threw a hairbrush and toothbrush in there also, plus I guess some basic makeup. Oh, I also called your parents last night and filled them in on what I knew. When we get back to town you can talk to them, and I think your fiancé might be there too. The roads are now open and they said that there was no way that they wouldn't be there when we brought you out and back to town. So we will have a brief stop at the café before you make your trip to the hospital to make sure that ankle wasn't broken, or that there might be some other hidden injury. So please take your time, we'll just sit here and talk with Will, and have some of his coffee. Besides I am sure he enjoys the company. We are in no hurry at all so please take as much time as you feel you need."

Almost unable to contain herself she laughed with delight, such a range of emotions today. Then carefully as she hadn't quite gotten the use of the crutches down yet she picked up the bag, and worked her way back into the bathroom. As she entered she asked. "Will, do you mind, or you TD if I take another shower before we head out. I'd feel much better."

Smiling again and shaking his head Will said, "Not a problem for me, and you TD?" Who just shook his head. Smiling, she hobbled into the bathroom. When she opened the bag the first thing she saw was a note from the sheriff's wife and it said. "Cathy, I know what you have been through is probably the toughest thing you've ever done. I've baked some chocolate chip cookies, which you will find in a bag in here. You know us women and chocolate. I've also enclosed a toothbrush, toothpaste, some shampoo and rinse, I for one am sure that your hair is a mess and this will help you get it straightened out, and of course a brush to make it easier. Looking at your clothes I would guess that you're a little smaller than I am, but I am also sure that you have no jacket to wear so here also is one that you can give TD when you reach town. There's some basic makeup also here. And I will be in town with your parents and loved ones so I can get a chance to meet you – someone who has beaten the odds and lived, but I suspect that you had help. Laura."

Reading this as she sat on the lid of the toilet brought the tears again. But this time it was tears of closure and of joy. Yet the part of the note that stated that Laura suspected that she had help she really did not understand. Cathy suspected that she knew the answer, but at this time wasn't sure if that was it or not. At this point she eagerly dug everything out of the bag and got to work.

* * *

It probably was close to an hour before she emerged from the bathroom feeling clean and maybe a little more feminine than she had for the past week. Still learning the crutches she hobbled over to them and said, "I guess I am just about as ready as I can be." Then looking around she saw the backpack that had been so much a part of her living that she wanted to make sure that it went with her. Will smiling said, "Figured you might want that, so I've put everything you had, other than what is in the bathroom in it. So I just need to add those dirty clothes. I even put the car seat material in there. Figured you could decide later what you wanted to do with it. Okay now go outside and join TD and Jacob, and I'll bring this out to you before you leave."

Once outside they assisted her into the sled that was attached to one of the snowmobiles, and then lightly strapped her in and made her comfortable. TD told her that it would be around an hour before they got to town as he was going to take it easy. Then Will brought out her pack and said to her, "Cathy it has been a pleasure. I think I would like to keep in contact with you. So I've put a couple of my business cards in the backpack. I think your story of your fight to survive all that you have will be an inspiration to others. So when you've had time to recover and to think about all that has happened please let's get together and see where you would like this to go. Now go back to your loved ones. I am sure they are eager to see you, especially alive. There had been so many times that it could have been otherwise. I believe that God has something important for you to do in your life. Anybody who could have been on the outside looking in would know that you were helped. Too many things had to come together to be coincidence." He then hugged her and then waved to TD to head on out. As he stood there he watched them until they were lost among the trees. Then turning around he said. "Well Sam. It's been an interesting end to winter. Guess it's time for us to pack up and head out ourselves. Won't be long and the roads into this area will be open again and we can get back to our other place." Sam then barked a joyful bark as if he understood all that had been said, and they both went back into the now empty cabin.

* * *

That day flew by faster than any she could remember. It was emotionally overwhelming when she and the sheriff arrived at the little café. To see her family filled with joy from her rescue, and to especially see Keith there with his family too. There were many tears of joy and some laughter as they were all together again. It was here where she met Laura, the sheriff's wife, and thanked her for her caring thoughts and deeds. Then came the trip to the hospital where they poked and prodded her, and pronounced that for having gone through what she had that she was in excellent shape. And no the ankle was not broken, but it was severely sprained.

Soon after returning home Cathy again began to go back to church with the family. It was during this time that the dream she had back when she was still in her wrecked car came to mind. She related the dream to the preacher, who stated that when one dealt with ladders or steps leading to heaven that these were messages from God. He went on to interpret it for her, and she had to admit it made total sense. After all only students and teachers – those who had accepted the gift Christ offered could go across that abyss. Then about two months later she made the altar call and accepted Christ as her personal savior. She had thought about it a lot and had gone over her days in the wilderness and had found that indeed for her to survive God would have had to have guided her footsteps. There was no other explanation. She had tried to explain it away many times but it always came back to God and his guiding hand. Then in a flash once again Psalm 23 came into her mind. "The

Lord is my Shepherd . . ." She then realized that indeed God had been there to protect her, and much of what was described in that Psalm had happened to her and he *had* protected her. During this time she and Keith continued planning for their wedding, and that June she became a bride. Something when she looked back to that time, and thought it would never happen once she had awakened in her wrecked car, and realized that she was all alone, and there was no one who had a clue where she was.

Epilog
15 Years Later

"Momma . . ." Audrey her 13-year-old daughter asked.

"Yes dear what is it?" The mother was sitting in the small reading room where they kept their books. It was Saturday and the 3 children were home. Audrey, the oldest then continued. "Momma, I know that I'm supposed to ask permission to take some of these books that you hold special. But I was always curious about this one." She held it out for her mother to see. She smiled back at her daughter. Even still it was a sad smile. She knew it immediately. Then Audrey continued. "I always wanted to read it, as for some reason, I've always been drawn to it. In the introduction it says that it's a true story." Audrey paused, before continuing, "A true story? After reading it, it just seems to be too much for anyone to have lived through. It's also signed by the author with a note, which states: 'To a close friend. May our friendship last a lifetime.'? Is he the writer who comes and visits us now and then?"

Again smiling her mother said, "Yes, the very one. We've been close for a very long time. We met before your father and I married. In a way you can say he was instrumental in making sure I was able to make that wedding."

"So momma, do you feel it's a true story? I know that you hold it dear."

"Yes, I found it to be quite a story." Here she paused a moment as if thinking. "Tell you what, this afternoon he will be coming over to visit. When he does, why not ask him yourself. I give you permission. I think he'll tell you what you want to know."

"Who's coming over this afternoon momma?"

Smiling while looking at Audrey she said, "Oh the one who wrote that book that you are holding there."

"Oh." Was just about all she could say. She wasn't sure if she wanted to ask or not. *But the story seems to be . . . well, it seemed that it had to be fiction. How could anyone have gone through all of that and live?*

A couple of hours later someone knocked on the door and Audrey's father went to answer. "Hey, long time no see, as always it's great to see you. So how's it all going?"

"Great as always Pastor, and I can see that all seems well as I expect." The writer said as he entered the cozy home. "I always feel so welcome here. It's one of the reasons I love visiting." Then turning to one side he continued, saying, "and hi lady of the house". He had a slight teasing in his voice as he watched her enter the living room. "You look great!"

"Well thank you. You always know how to please a woman. By the way, when you get settled, Audrey wants to ask you something about one of the books you wrote. She'll be a little shy but she is curious."

Audrey, standing in the hallway heard what her mother had said and kind of tentatively nodded. "I do have a question sir, but it can wait."

"Sir is it? No, that's all right Audrey, what is it?" He asked, now curious himself.

"Are you sure? I mean I don't want to interrupt what you, mom and dad want to talk about."

Glancing around to the other two then at Audrey he said, "No just go ahead and ask. I'm here through dinner so I'll have plenty of time to catch up. Tell you what let's go over to the couch and then you can ask. Does that work for you?"

With her hands together and wringing them somewhat, plus she was staring at the floor as she mumbled. "Yes."

Smiling he said. "Okay come on I'm sure it's important to you." As he sat down on the couch he patted the seat inviting her to do the same. When both were sitting on the couch, with him facing Audrey, he asked. "Okay what's so important?"

"Well, I read your book, this one right here, and in the introduction it says that this is a true story." Pausing for a moment not quite sure how to state what she wanted, she hesitantly continued. "I felt that what this person went through, well she couldn't have lived through it. So some of it is made up right?"

Pausing for a moment and then looking up at Audrey's mother questioningly he saw her nod that he could continue. Seeing the interaction between her mother and her mother's friend, Audrey didn't quite know what to think. "Okay Audrey, I just got permission to tell you. This story is true, and nothing in it is made up or embellished. You see the woman in the story; the woman who lived through that ordeal, and faced all those many challenges of life and death is your mother. She is *The Woman in the Snow*."

F.D. Brant always wanted to write, but life got in the way. Finally after retiring he got his chance.

Storytelling and writing has always been F.D. Brant's passion, but responsibilities took preference. And because of those responsibilities it took retiring to allow those passions to come to fruition. Since retiring he has written 9 books, and maintains a weekly eclectic blog, Words in the Wind.

Growing up in the backcountry he learned the appreciation of "doing things for yourself". Because it was impossible to call in someone to repair anything one either did it themselves or went without. This led to the appreciation of the natural world, and the daily struggles that one faced as nature threw problems at the family that had to be overcome, leading to confidence and self-sufficiency. This led to the strong characters that populate his stories and books. And his female protagonists are strong willed and confident – something that he saw in both in his mother and sister.